Puffin Books

Chocolate Porridge
AND
OTHER STORIES

Here are twenty-one marvellously inventive stories by an outstanding children's writer, irresistibly illustrated by Shirley Hughes.

From Christopher's 'Horrible Story', which terrifies two older boys, to Timothy's special 'Chocolate Porridge'; from 'The Curiosity Concert' to 'The Girl Who Loved Cars', each of these enchanting stories will delight, surprise and amuse.

Margaret Mahy is a New Zealander who has been writing stories from the age of seven. She has won the Carnegie Medal twice. Her books for Puffin include *Raging Robots and Unruly Uncles*, *The Little Witch and 5 Other Favourites* and *The Boy Who Bounced and Other Magic Tales*. Margaret Mahy has two grown-up daughters, several cats and thousands of books. She lives near Christchurch, South Island, in a house she partly built herself.

Other books by Margaret Mahy

Chocolate Porridge
AND
OTHER STORIES

Margaret Mahy

Illustrated by Shirley Hughes

Puffin Books

PUFFIN BOOKS

Published by the Penguin Group
27 Wrights Lane, London W8 5TZ, England
Viking Penguin Inc., 40 West 23rd Street, New York, New York 10010, USA
Penguin Books Australia Ltd, Ringwood, Victoria, Australia
Penguin Books Canada Ltd, 2801 John Street, Markham,
Ontario, Canada L3R 1B4
Penguin Books (NZ) Ltd, 182–190 Wairau Road,
Auckland 10, New Zealand

Penguin Books Ltd, Registered Offices: Harmondsworth,
Middlesex, England

First published by J. M. Dent & Sons Ltd 1987
Published in Puffin Books 1989
1 3 5 7 9 10 8 6 4 2

From *The First Margaret Mahy Story Book*
'The Playground', 'The Letter', 'The Tick-Tock Party', 'The Boy Who Went Looking
for a Friend', 'The Little Boy Who Wanted a Flat World', 'The Strange Egg'

From *The Second Margaret Mahy Story Book*
'The Horrible Story', 'A Present From Star', 'Mrs Bartelmy's Pet', 'Chocolate
Porridge', 'Telephone Detectives', 'The Adventures of Little Mouse', 'Patrick Comes
to School', 'The Butterfly Garden', 'Billy Thring', 'Tom Tib Goes Shopping'

From *The Third Margaret Mahy Story Book*
'The Breakfast Bird', 'The Curiosity Concert', 'The Girl Who Loved Cars', 'The
Trees', 'A Tall Story'

Printed in Great Britain by
Cox and Wyman Ltd, Reading, Berks

Filmset in 11/13 pt Linotron Sabon by
Rowland Phototypesetting Ltd,
Bury St Edmunds, Suffolk

Contents

The Horrible Story

Outside it was quite dark, but inside the boys had a candle-lantern which cast a pale, flickering light on the tawny sides of the tent. You could not see much – only the long shapes of sleeping-bags and blankets, and the humpy shapes of heads and pillows.

The two longest shapes were Robert and Allan, who were by the door flap, which was fastened back tonight. They had told Christopher, Robert's little brother, that they wanted to look out into the garden and watch the stars, but really they had their own secret reasons for wanting to be together by the door, and for making him sleep on his own at the back of the tent. *His* bedtime shape was just blankets, for he had no sleeping-bag, and it was a shorter shape than Allan's or Robert's, because he was only small – not quite seven – and they were ten.

Yesterday morning there had been no tent. A large parcel had arrived at lunch time addressed to Mr Robert and Mr Christopher Johnson. Robert's eyes had shone with surprise and delight when it had been opened, and its layers of paper and cardboard peeled back. It was a tent – not just a white tent such as you might see in any camp-ground either, but a tawny-brown tent that could belong to an Indian or an outlaw or some wild, fierce hero.

There had been the fun of fitting the poles together and putting it up at the bottom of the garden, sheltered by the hedge, and the sudden excitement when they realized that they would be allowed to sleep out all night in it.

'Can Allan come too, Mum?' asked Robert, because Allan was his best friend, and they always shared adventures.

'Of course he may, if he is allowed,' Mother replied, smiling.

'Me too!' Christopher cried anxiously, for he knew that when Allan and Robert were together he was always just a little brother to be left behind or taken no notice of. 'It's *my* tent too, isn't it?'

Robert looked at him rather sourly. He said, 'You can come some other time. You've got lots of chances.'

His mother turned round sharply.

'Now, don't be difficult, Bob!' she said. 'Of course Christopher can camp out too. If there's no room for Christopher there's no room for Allan either.'

So here they were, the three of them, Allan and Robert, and Christopher on his own in the back of the tent, looking a bit lonely and small in the flickering shadows.

Secretly Allan nudged Robert as a sign that he was going to begin the Get-rid-of-Christopher plan . . . a plan they had made that afternoon riding their bicycles home from the river.

'Little kids get scared easy as easy in the dark,' Allan had said, his wet, red hair standing on end, his green eyes narrowed against the wind. He had glanced behind to see if Christopher was listening. The little boy had had his usual dreamy look and was practising his whistling. 'I bet when your little brother hears one of my famous horrible tales he'll run inside to Mummy and won't want to come into the tent ever again. Then we'll have a midnight feast, eh? I'll bring a tin of fruit salad, and a tin opener, and some luncheon sausage.'

'I'll buy a packet of biscuits,' Robert had replied. 'I've got ten pence.'

As he remembered this he slid his hand under the pillow to feel the biscuits he'd hidden there. The paper crackled, and Christopher turned his head a little bit. Quickly Robert nudged Allan to show that he understood the plan was beginning. Allan blew out the candle in the lantern and for a moment everything went black as the night came, silent and sudden, into the tent.

'Hey,' said Allan, 'I know a story. It's pretty ghostly though . . .' He let his voice fade away uncertainly.

'Go on!' Robert said. 'Tell us! I'm not scared.'

'I'm not scared either,' said Christopher's piping voice from the back of the tent. He did not sound the least bit like a wild, fierce hero though.

'It's good you're not scared,' Allan declared,

'because it's a really horrible story, and it's about a boy called Christopher too. Now listen!

'This boy called Christopher lived in an old, dark house on the edge of a big forest. The forest was old too, and dark, like this tent, and full of creepy noises. Sometimes people went in, but no one ever came out again. Lots of rats lived in this forest, big as cats . . .' Allan paused, thinking out the next bit. In the little silence Robert was amazed to hear Christopher's small voice come in unexpectedly.

'When those rats ran around,' he said, 'their feet made a rustly sound, didn't they?' Outside, the hedge rustled in the wind, and Christopher added, '. . . a bit like that.'

'Huh!' said Allan crossly. 'And I suppose you think you know what else lived in the forest?'

'Yes . . . yes, I do, Allan.'

'Look, who's telling this story?' cried Allan indignantly. Then he asked rather cautiously, 'Well, what else *did* live there?'

'Spiders,' said Christopher. 'Big hairy spiders . . . big as footballs . . . but hairy all over like dish mops, huge black dish mops going scuttle, scuttle on lots of thin legs –'

Allan interrupted him fiercely, 'Hey shut *up*, will you! This is my story, isn't it? Well then . . . there weren't any spiders, but there was a dragon.'

Allan went on talking about the bigness and smokiness of the dragon, but Robert felt disappointed in it. Somehow it did not seem nearly as frightening as the scuttling, hairy spiders. On the other side of the tent something went *tap*, *tap*, *tap!* like quick little feet running over the canvas. Allan stopped and listened.

'It's just the wind,' Christopher said in a kind voice. 'It's just a scraping, twiggy piece from the hedge. Go on, Allan.'

Robert suddenly felt sorry for Christopher, lying there so trustingly staring into the dark with round black eyes like shoe buttons. Christopher was just not an adventurer. He was not the sort of boy who knew anything about the wild scaring life of the wide world. Christopher was the sort who would rather stay at home and read fairy stories than plan wars in the gorse or battles over the sand hills. Perhaps it was a bit mean to frighten him out of the tent, a tent which was really half his.

'Never mind!' thought Robert. 'He'll have lots of other chances.' Under his pillow the biscuit paper crackled faintly.

'And then, one night . . .' Allan said mysteriously, 'the little boy was on his own in the old house when . . . guess what happened?'

'Somebody knocked at the door,' said Christopher promptly. 'Three knocks, very slowly, KNOCK KNOCK KNOCK, like that.'

'Fair go!' replied Allan scornfully. 'Do you know who it was, Mr Smart?'

'Yes,' Christopher went on, 'the little boy opened the door and there was a man there all in black, at least it looked like a man, but you couldn't tell really, because he had a black thing over his face, a black silk scarf thing. And do you know what he said? He said, "Little boy, the time has come for you to follow *me*."' Christopher stopped, and the tent was quiet except for the sad-sea sound of the wind.

'Did the boy go?' asked Robert. He did not want to ask, but suddenly he felt he had to know.

Allan said nothing. Christopher's voice was almost dreamy, as he replied,

'Yes, he did. He just couldn't help it. And as he went out of the door it shut itself behind him. The gate did too. Then they were in that forest. Everywhere was the rustling noise of rats and spiders.'

'Hey . . .' began Allan.

'What?' squeaked Christopher. Allan turned over restlessly in the dark.

'Nothing! Go on!' he said.

'And *things* followed them,' Christopher went on, making his voice deep and mysterious. 'The man went first, and the boy followed the man, and if he looked back he saw things with *eyes* coming after him, but he couldn't see what things they were.'

'What were they?' asked Robert in a small voice.

'Just things!' said Christopher solemnly. 'Spooky things . . . with little red eyes,' he added thoughtfully. 'Then they came to a clearing place – there was a fire burning – not a yellow fire though, a blue one. All the flames were blue. It looked *ghastly*!' cried Christopher, pleased with his grown-up word. 'There were three heads – just heads, no arms or legs or bodies or anything – sticking out of the ground round the fire.' He stopped again. Allan and Robert could hear their own breathing. They did not ask any questions and Christopher went on with his story again. 'They were ugly, UGLY heads and they had these smiles on their faces' – Christopher was trying to think of words bad enough to describe the smiles – 'more horrible than anything you ever saw. They were yellow too, mind you, like cheese. One head looked at the man with cruel, mean eyes and said,

'"So you brought us some food."

'The man replied, "Yes, and it's very tender tonight."

'"Well, it's just as well," the head said, "or we'd have had to eat *you*."

'Then the second head said, "We'll have a good tuck-in tonight, eh, brothers? Bags I be the one to drink his blood." Then the third head opened its mouth, wide as wide, like a cat yawning, you know, and it had all these pointy teeth, like needles, some short and some long, and it didn't even say anything. It just began to scream, horrible, high-up screams . . .'

Christopher's voice got louder and higher with excitement, and at this very moment, almost it seemed at Robert's ear, a shrill furious howl arose from under the hedge. Allan scrambled to his feet with a cry of terror and went hopping madly out of the tent, too frightened to get out of his sleeping-bag first.

'The head!' yelled Robert and followed him, so frightened he felt sick and shaky in his stomach. Under the hedge were heads with teeth like needles waiting to bite him up as if he was an apple.

Christopher was alone in the tent. Quickly he hopped from under his blankets and stuck his head out through the tent flap. He saw Allan and Robert, still zipped in their sleeping-bags, hopping and stumbling up the lawn.

'It ends happily!' he shouted.

Then he thoughtfully put his hand under Allan's pillow and helped himself to the luncheon sausage hidden there.

Voices were talking on the veranda.

'It was only a cat fight!' Christopher's father was saying. 'Great Scott, if you're going to be scared by a cat fight, we'll never make campers of you.'

Christopher grinned to himself in the dark and quietly felt for the biscuits under Robert's pillow.

A Present From Star

When winter came there were frosty mornings, and the cold began to nip Penny's knees.

'My feet are warm in their socks and the rest of me is warm too,' she said, 'but my knees are in between, and the cold gets them, Mummy.'

'Well,' said Mummy, 'we'll have to do something about that,' and she did not forget. She bought Penny a pair of green tights. They looked like long green stockings when Penny wore them and felt very warm and comfy indeed. Penny liked putting them on every morning.

'No more cold knees now I've got these green grasshopper legs,' she said. 'I love wearing these tights, Mummy.'

'Well,' said Mummy, 'they look very cosy, but you're getting them a bit dirty. They'll have to be washed tomorrow if it is fine.'

The next day was fine and sunny.

'Your tights will be dry in no time,' said Mummy as she pegged them out. They looked like funny green legs kicking on the line in the winter wind.

Penny and her mother went in to make lunch. Penny watched the toast and did not burn a single piece. After lunch the sun went in behind

the clouds and it began to get really cold again.

'Mummy, can I go to the line and see if my tights are dry?' Penny asked.

'Well,' said Mummy, 'I don't expect they will be yet, but you never know with a good wind . . . go and see if you like.'

Off ran Penny down the path to the clothes-line. She looked for her tights and then stared in amazement. There they were, dangling on the line, but they didn't look like tights any more, they didn't look like anything except rags. The feet were gone, the knees were gone. Penny could not understand it. What could have happened to her tights? Then an unexpected voice said:

'*Mehhhhh!*'

Penny jumped in fright and turned round. There, under the spindleberry tree, was a white animal with horns and a beard. It blinked yellow eyes at her and said '*Mehhhh!*' again. It was Mrs Simon's goat, Star.

Penny had often seen Star over Mrs Simon's fence eating the grassy bits of Mrs Simon's garden.

She was suddenly scared of those yellow eyes and curling horns. She ran back up the path calling, 'Mummy, Mummy!' as loudly as she could.

As she came up the path she was pleased to see Mrs Simon herself standing on the step with a collar and chain in her hand.

Penny guessed she was looking for Star.

'Star's here!' she called. 'Star's here, eating my tights.'

Mrs Simon and Mummy ran down the path, and Penny ran close behind them. Star was nibbling the bushes. She stopped and looked at them. Her horns looked curlier than ever.

'That's my naughty Star,' said Mrs Simon. She held out an apple and Star came daintily over to get it.

'Won't she horn us?' Penny asked nervously.

'No, she's very tame,' said Mrs Simon. 'But she is greedy too. She must have liked the green look of your tights.'

'She's even eaten the knees!' said Penny.

'Never mind!' said Mummy. 'It's been an adventure for us, hasn't it? It isn't every day we have a goat visitor. Can you tie her up to the garage door perhaps, Mrs Simon, and come in and have a cup of tea?'

'Santa Claus has a beard like Star's,' Penny said as Mrs Simon put a collar round Star's neck, 'but no horns.'

'He doesn't eat the washing either,' said Mrs Simon.

The next day, when Penny came home from play centre, there was a parcel waiting for her. She opened it, very excited, and found inside it *two* pairs of tights, a green pair and a red pair. There was a card with them that said, 'A present to Penny.' Then at the bottom it said, 'Those other tights were most delicious! With love from Goat Star.'

The Breakfast Bird

'Look!' said Johnny. 'Look at Cathie's toast!'

Everyone looked at Cathie's toast.

'Oh, Cathie!' said their mother. 'You've done it again. There is honey everywhere.'

There was honey all over Cathie's toast.

There was honey all over Cathie's plate.

There was honey all over Cathie's face.

'You have even got it on the tablecloth,' said their mother.

'Well, I like honey,' said Cathie. 'I like *plenty* of honey.'

'You are a greedy honey bear,' said their mother. 'Most of that honey will be wasted.'

'Not if I lick my plate out in the kitchen,' replied Cathie. 'It won't be wasted then.'

'Bad manners though!' said Mack, the eldest of the children.

'It isn't bad manners out in the kitchen,' argued Johnny. 'Licking plates is only bad manners at the table.'

This was a family rule.

'As long as she doesn't try to lick the tablecloth,' Mack answered in a grunty voice. Things began to quieten down. Then Johnny began again.

'Mum, you know Mr Cooney's budgie has hatched out babies.'

'No, how should I know?' said Johnny's mother. 'You've only told me twenty times already.' She was trying to scrape honey off the tablecloth as she spoke.

'Well, can't I have one? Please, *please*!' begged Johnny. 'I'd teach it to talk and perch on my finger. Mr Cooney's budgie perches on his finger.'

'Yes, you might teach it to perch,' said his mother, 'but would you remember to give it fresh water? Would you clean out its cage and make sure it had plenty of seed every day? I don't think you would.'

'Yes, I would!' Johnny cried quickly, his eyes blue and startled in his freckled face. 'I'd help in the garden too. Budgies like something fresh and green every day.'

Johnny's mother laughed.

'I'll tell you what . . .' she said at last. 'Today, Cathie's Play Centre group finishes for the holidays. The mothers have to take the pets home and feed them and look after them until the Play Centre begins again. Shall I bring the budgie home? Then we can just see how good you are at looking after a budgie.'

'He's a nice budgie,' called Cathie. 'His name is Nippy because he tries to bite our fingers.'

'If he bit your finger,' said Mack, 'he'd get a beakful of honey. His beak would be all stuck up for hours.'

When Johnny came home from school the next day his mother said, 'There's a visitor in the sitting-room.'

'Yes,' Cathie cried like a squeaky echo, 'there's a green visitor sitting on the table.'

The green visitor was Nippy, the Play Centre budgie.

Johnny wanted a blue budgie, not a green one.

He went up to the Play Centre cage and looked at Nippy.

Nippy looked back at Johnny from little black eyes. Nippy looked like a small round-shouldered pirate. He looked like a goblin in a green shawl. He shuffled along his perch, six steps left, six steps right. Then he hooked his beak over the wire of the cage, crawled up the wire and hung upside-down on the roof.

'Will he sit on my finger?' asked Johnny.

'Well, he's very tame,' said Johnny's mother, 'but I don't want you to open the big door of his cage at all. Remember he isn't ours. It would be a great pity to lose him.'

Every morning Johnny gave Nippy fresh water. Every morning Johnny checked Nippy's bird-seed.

'Johnny! Johnny!' called Johnny's mother. 'Where have you got to?'

'I'm just getting Nippy some sow thistle,' came Johnny's voice from a weedy part of the garden.

'Hey, Johnny, where are you?' shouted Mack.

'Cutting a piece of apple for Nippy,' answered Johnny from the kitchen.

Every three days Johnny cleaned out Nippy's cage. He wanted to show his mother just how well he could look after a budgie.

'Johnny, where are you?' cried Cathie down the hall.

'Talking to Nippy!' Johnny called back. 'I

don't want him to be lonely while he's having his holidays.'

'I'm glad the Play Centre pet isn't an owl,' remarked Johnny's father. 'We'd have Johnny up all night catching mice for it.'

The holidays went by quickly.

'You've taken such good care of Nippy that I think we could let you have a blue budgie,' Johnny's mother said. 'We'll go and see Mr Cooney about it tomorrow.'

The first day of the new school term came round.

Johnny was trying to keep his clean first-morning-of-school clothes tidy and give Nippy fresh seed. Nippy ran backwards and forwards on his perch. His feet were wrinkled and grey, with three toes going forward and one toe going back. Once Mr Cooney had let Johnny put his hand into the Cooney budgie's cage and a blue Cooney budgie had settled on his finger. Its feet, which looked horny and cold, were light and warm. It had shuffled and bobbed and winked at Johnny.

Suddenly he wanted, very much, to feel those light warm feet again.

There was no one in the room but Cathie, and she was not watching him. Instead she was arranging her breakfast, spreading a great spoonful of honey on her toast. It took only a moment to open the big door of the cage. Johnny slid his hand in and pressed a clean first-morning-of-school finger against Nippy's green chest. Nippy stepped on to Johnny's finger. His grey feet were just as small and light as Johnny remembered.

Slowly Nippy walked over Johnny's hand, going sideways with his head tilted. Then, he did a quick little dance, and before Johnny knew what was happening Nippy had slid up across his wrist and out of the cage door. His wings fluttered wildly. Nippy was flying round and round the room, and there was nothing Johnny could do but stand and stare. Cathie stared too. Two pairs of round blue eyes followed the green budgie round and round and round. Nippy landed on the cord of the electric light. He hung there staring back at them. It was terrible. In another moment Johnny knew his mother would come in. She would know that Johnny had opened the big door of the Play Centre cage and had let the Play Centre budgie out. There would be no blue Cooney budgie for Johnny unless Nippy could be caught and returned to his cage before Play Centre time.

Nippy took off again, whirring round the room. He flew lower this time and settled on the curtain rail.

'Climb on a chair and catch him,' breathed Cathie. Johnny scrambled on to a chair, but before his hand was anywhere near Nippy off Nippy flew, round and round and round. His wings made a busy breathing sound in the still room. Johnny began to run backwards and for-

wards beneath him. Nippy flew lower and lower
and lower as if his wings were getting tired. He
landed on the table.

'Johnny!' cried Cathie. Nippy had landed on
her piece of toast.

The toast was thickly spread with honey.

Nippy could not get his feet out of it.

In a moment Johnny had caught him again.
Holding him very gently he wiped Nippy's tiny
honey feet with his clean first-day-of-school
handkerchief. When most of the honey was off he

slipped the little bird back into the Play Centre cage.

'Gosh!' mumbled Cathie, staring at her toast. 'I don't think this toast is good any more. I thought it was salt you had to put on the tail for catching birds.'

'Honey on the feet is better,' said Johnny, beginning to grin again, though the grin felt stiff on his face as if it was a new one he was wearing for the first time.

'Should we tell?' asked Cathie.

'If anyone asks we have to tell,' Johnny answered carefully.

Cathie nodded to herself.

'No one will ask,' she murmured, and began licking her sticky fingers.

The door opened and their mother came in.

'Haven't you finished yet?' she cried.

'I have really,' said Cathie. 'The trouble was – too much toast.'

'Put it in the hen's dish in the kitchen,' said mother. 'The hens will love it.'

'They'd better not stand on it,' said Cathie very seriously.

A minute later they were ready to go. Mother and Cathie were off to Play Centre. Mack and Johnny were off to school. Mother was carrying Nippy in his Play Centre cage. Just as they were about to step off Nippy looked through the bars of his cage at Johnny.

'Johnny!' he shouted, 'Johnny! Johnny! Johnny! Where are you?'

'Oh!' gasped Johnny. 'He called me. He called my name.'

'Oh dear!' said Johnny's mother. 'Just what do we do now?'

For Johnny suddenly knew that he did not want a blue Cooney budgie after all. He wanted

Nippy, that wicked green Nippy, who could call his name. His mother seemed to understand this, for she smiled and then began to laugh a little bit.

'Off to school,' she said. 'We'll talk about it after school.'

When Johnny came home that afternoon a voice shouted at him as soon as he came into the room.

'Johnny! Johnny! Where's Johnny!'

Nippy was in his usual place as green and dancing as ever. However, he had a new cage, even larger than the Play Centre one, with a swing and two seed boxes.

His feet were covered in seed husks.

'He's wearing boots,' said Cathie. Her round blue eyes were smiling. 'Mum bought a blue Cooney budgie for the Play Centre so we are allowed to keep Nippy for always. Aren't you pleased?'

'Of course I am,' Johnny answered. 'He is the one I wanted after all.'

'He can come out of his cage and fly around the room now he's a member of the family,' Cathie went on.

'If we can work out how to catch him again,' said their mother, 'though he is so tame he will usually go back to his cage himself after a while.'

'No need to worry anyway, Mum,' said Johnny, beginning to laugh. 'Cathie could catch him in her breakfast bird trap.'

And with Nippy listening and shouting encouragement Johnny and Cathie began to tell their mother about the honey-and-budgie-breakfast adventures.

Mrs Bartelmy's Pet

High on a hill in her pointed house lived fierce little Mrs Bartelmy, who had once been a pirate queen. She lived there on her own with her gold earrings and wooden leg, and a box of treasure buried in her garden under the sunflowers.

Though she was fierce, Mrs Bartelmy often felt lonely. She was used to having lots of adventures. She was used to the gay, wicked conversation of pirates. Now she lived on her own she often wished for someone to talk to.

'I could get a cat,' thought Mrs Bartelmy, 'but they are tame, sleepy animals. I am such a fierce old woman my cat would probably be scared of me. I wish I had been just a granny and not a pirate queen. Then a cat would love me.'

Mrs Bartelmy was fond of sunflowers. She planted them all round her house. They grew so tall they almost hid the roof. One day when Mrs Bartelmy was digging among them she found the biggest cat she had ever seen sleeping there. It was a yellow cat with a small waist and tufted tail, and Mrs Bartelmy liked it at once. It had a golden mane round its face that reminded her of sunflowers. It yawned and showed its red mouth and white teeth. Then it smiled at Mrs Bartelmy.

Mrs Bartelmy went and brought it a big bowl of milk and a string of sausages. The cat lapped the milk. It ate all the sausages and growled fiercely.

'That's the boy!' said Mrs Bartelmy. 'I like a chap who enjoys his food. You're fierce enough for me and I'm fierce enough for you. We'll get along together like a couple of jolly shipmates.'

At that moment the gate squeaked. Mrs Bartelmy went to see who was coming. It was four men with huge nets and a fat man with a whip.

'We are circus men looking for our lion,' said one of the men.

'The wicked, ungrateful animal has run away,'

said the fat man. 'I am Signor Rosetta the Lion Tamer.' He cracked his whip.

At the sound of the whip the big yellow cat leaped out, roaring furiously. Mrs Bartelmy's big cat was a lion!

'You aren't to chase this lion,' said Mrs Bartelmy. 'He's a half-fierce, half-friendly lion and he's my shipmate.'

'Well, you could have him,' said Signor Rosetta, 'but we need him for the circus, and we haven't got enough money to buy another lion.'

'Is that all your worry?' said Mrs Bartelmy. She took her spade to a secret corner of her sunflower garden and dug up her chest of pirate treasure. She gave the lion tamer two handfuls of diamonds and Indian rubies.

'Is this enough to buy him?' she asked.

The lion tamer was delighted.

'It is enough to get three lions and two Bengal tigers. Ours will be the fiercest circus in the world!' he cried.

He went away and made the men with the nets go with him.

'That's that,' said Mrs Bartelmy. Once the lion tamer, his whip and his nets were gone, the lion became gentle again and smiled at Mrs Bartelmy. It had flowers in its mane and smelled of new hay.

'Well, I never thought to get a cat so much to my liking,' said Mrs Bartelmy. 'I won't have to worry about scaring it when I get fierce, and it matches my sunflowers.'

The lion and Mrs Bartelmy lived happily ever after. Often I have passed them, sitting on the doorstep of their pointed house among the sunflowers, singing with all their might:

Oh, there was an old woman
 who lived on her own
In a little house made from a smooth
 white bone.
And she sat at her door with a
 barrel of beer,
And a bright gold ring in her old
 brown ear.
And folk who passed by her
 they always agreed,
That's a queer little,
 wry little,
 fierce little,
 spry little,
Utterly strange little
 woman indeed.

Chocolate
Porridge
(and who ate it)

One Friday afternoon Timothy's mother was cooking, cooking for the weekend.

Timothy's two big sisters Pink and Sally were allowed to help her, but Timothy had to go outside.

'The kitchen isn't big enough for everyone,' said Timothy's mother.

'I want to cook too,' he said, frowning and scuffling his red sneakers.

'Boys don't cook!' said Sally.

'Boys can't cook,' said Pink.

Timothy was filled with giant indignation.

'Some boys cook!' he cried. 'John's big brother got First Prize for gingerbread at the flower show.'

'It isn't just that you are a boy,' Pink told him. 'You are too small to be a cook.'

'You are too little to be anything serious,' said Sally.

She smoothed her blue apron with smug pink hands.

Timothy had to go outside.

Outside on the terrace the sun was splashing the stones with hot gold. At the end of the terrace, against the wall, were the garden tools, the rake and the two hoes, the blunt spade and the pointed dibble.

There was the lawn-mower waiting to clash its teeth in the grass. There was a row of flowerpots. Timothy's father was painting inside the toolshed, and all the tools were camping out on the terrace.

One big pottery bowl caught his eye. It looked like a mixing-bowl. Timothy pulled it out into the middle of the terrace and looked at it. Where the garden had been newly dug, the ground was soft and fine. It reminded Timothy of grated chocolate.

He thought it looked delicious.

Digging at the edge with a trowel, Timothy put grated chocolate garden dirt into his pottery bowl. He rubbed his hands in it. 'It's got to be fine,' he said to himself. 'They *like* it fine.'

'What *are* you doing?' asked Sally in her bossiest voice. She had come out on to the terrace behind him. She put her hands on her hips and her head on one side like a grown-up.

'I'm beginning to mix something,' Timothy answered in a secret voice. He wouldn't look up to her.

'Mixing what?' she asked.

'Something!' Timothy answered. 'I don't have to tell you.'

He rubbed his hands in the chocolate dirt and felt very powerful.

A moment later he heard Sally's high voice in the kitchen saying, 'Timothy thinks he is mixing something real that someone will like.'

'I suppose it's just the same old mud pie,' said Pink with a laugh.

'Now, girls – remember he is just a little boy,' said their mother.

Timothy sneered to himself about all of them.

'They don't *know* what I'm making,' he muttered. 'It's going to be something good – something unusual – an unusual sort of porridge.'

A nearby lemon tree had lawn clippings around its roots.

Timothy added a few trowels full of grass clippings to the pottery bowl. He rubbed them into the chocolate dirt until you could scarcely see them.

'Cooking, cooking, cooking!' sang Timothy to himself.

'Some cooking!' cried Pink in scorn. She had come to shake flour from her apron. 'You're a mere mud-pie cook!'

'This isn't a mud pie,' replied Timothy. 'It is something special. It is chocolate porridge.'

'Chocolate nothing!' said Pink. 'It is a nothing! A big dirty nothing!'

Timothy let his mouth smile mysteriously at the corners.

'It *is* something,' he said. 'It is the famous chocolate porridge.'

Pink went inside.

'He says he is making chocolate porridge,' she said to Sally.

Timothy had followed her in.

40

'Could I have some salt?' he asked. 'They like it salty.'

'Who do?' asked Sally.

Timothy tried his mysterious smile again.

'I don't have to say,' he replied, looking sideways away from her.

Timothy's mother gave him some salt in a plastic cup.

Timothy went out on to the terrace again.

Soon the white grains of salt were lost in the brown chocolate porridge.

'Now the water!' muttered Timothy.

He filled the watering-can at the garden tap, and sprinkled water into his chocolate dirt, grass clipping and salt mixture. He stirred it lightly with the garden trowel and then sprinkled again.

'Sprinkle and Stir! Sprinkle and Stir!' sang Timothy. 'That's how they like it. Sprinkle and Stir.'

He stirred with the garden trowel.

There came a good cooking smell from the kitchen. It overflowed down the passage on to the terrace.

Timothy sniffed his own bowl with its earth and water and grass clippings and salt. It had a nice smell of its own, but it was a gardening smell, not an eating smell.

'They like it that way,' he said, stirring a little bit more.

Timothy looked at his chocolate porridge. He

liked its colour. He even liked its smell. But he did not really want to eat it himself.

'Some people like it like this,' he muttered, but he did not know what people. He thought hard, but he could not think of anyone who would enjoy his chocolate porridge.

There were quick, heavy steps round the side of the house. Timothy's father came on to the terrace.

'Turned out, are you?' said his father, smiling. 'You're lucky. There is a terrible mess in the kitchen. Women everywhere.'

'I've been mixing too,' said Timothy. 'Look! I've made chocolate porridge.'

His father looked at it. His eyebrows arched with surprise.

'So you have!' his father said. 'My word, it's years since I've seen chocolate porridge like that. It's very good. It's – I don't know how to put it – so fine, so well mixed. You've made a good job of it, I'd say. Do you think it needs just a little more water, perhaps?'

Timothy stirred and sprinkled.

'But, Dad,' he whispered, 'who will eat it? Pink and Sally have been bossing all afternoon, and I said someone would eat the chocolate porridge, but now I can't think who would eat it.'

'It just happens,' said his father, 'that, today of all days, I can help you. I've brought a permanent paying guest home with me. This guest is in the back of the car and I think he will love that chocolate porridge. It is just what he needs. Let's go round the side of the house. No need to let the women know what we're up to.'

The permanent paying guest was taller than Timothy and had green leaves. It was a garden tree, an apple tree. It held out its branches like little stiff arms.

'Pleased to meet you,' said Timothy, shaking hands.

'Chocolate porridge. I need chocolate porridge,' sighed the apple tree, or Timothy thought that it did.

Then Timothy and his father carried the apple tree down the garden and, while Timothy went to and fro collecting the spade, and carrying down the chocolate porridge and the watering-can full of water, his father changed into his old trousers.

Together they dug a suitable hole. Then they untied the sacking from round the apple tree's roots. They put the tree in the hole and Timothy was the one who spread the roots out, and poured the chocolate porridge all over them.

The chocolate porridge made a very chocolatey-porridgy slapping sound as it fell round the apple tree's anxious roots.

'Doesn't it sound delicious?' said Timothy's father. 'It almost makes me wish I was an apple tree.'

Then they filled the hole in. Timothy, having had a lot of practice, was allowed to sprinkle with the watering-can. His father trod the earth down

round the apple tree's trunk. They drove a garden stake in beside the tree and tied it so that the tree could lean on it if a wind blew.

They had just finished when Timothy's mother, and Pink and Sally, came down the path and looked over the hedge.

'Oh, wonderful! An apple tree!' said Timothy's mother.

'Yes,' said Timothy, 'and what do you think it's eating right now, at this very exact moment?'

'I don't know,' said his mother.

'Its roots are sucking up chocolate porridge,'

cried Timothy in great triumph. 'Trees love chocolate porridge.'

Pink and Sally looked at each other.

'Just think – salty apples,' said Pink, grinning.

'I didn't think of a cooking day for trees,' said Sally. 'It would be fun.'

'Next time we'll swap over,' said Timothy's father. 'The girls can help in the garden.'

'And Timothy can learn to cook scones,' said Timothy's mother.

When they went in for tea, Sally's biscuits were rather pale, and Pink's biscuits were rather dark. But out in the garden the apple tree thought Timothy's chocolate porridge was just about right.

The Playground

Just where the river curled out to meet the sea was the town playground, and next to the playground in a tall cream-coloured house lived Linnet. Every day after school she stood for a while at her window watching the children over the fence, and longing to run out and join them. She could hear the squeak squeak of the swings going up and down, up and down all afternoon. She could see children bending their knees pushing themselves up into the sky. She would think to herself, 'Yes, I'll go down now. I won't stop to think about it. I'll run out and have a turn on the slide,' but then she would feel her hands getting hot and her stomach shivery, and she knew she was frightened again.

Jim her brother and Alison her sister (who was a year younger than Linnet) were not frightened of the playground. Alison could fly down the slide with her arms held wide, chuckling as she went. Jim would spin on the roundabout until he felt more like a top than a boy, then he would jump off and roll over in the grass shouting with laughter. But when Linnet went on the slide the smooth shiny wood burned the backs of her legs, and she shot off the end so fast she tumbled over and made all the other children laugh. When she went on the roundabout the trees and the sky smudged

46

into one another and she felt sick. Even the swings frightened her and she held their chains so tightly that the links left red marks in her hands.

'Why should I be so scared?' she wondered. 'If only I could get on to the swing and swing without thinking about it I'd be all right. Only babies fall off. I wouldn't mind being frightened of lions or wolves but it is terrible to be frightened of swings and seesaws.'

Then a strange thing happened. Linnet's mother forgot to pull the blind down one night. The window was open and a little wind came in smelling of the ropes and tar on the wharf and of the salt sea beyond. Linnet sighed in her sleep and turned over. Then the moon began to set lower in the sky. It found her window and looked in at her. Linnet woke up.

The moonlight made everything quite different and enchanted. The river was pale and smooth and its other bank, the sandpit around which it twisted to find the sea, was absolutely black. The playground which was so noisy and crowded by day was deserted. It looked strange because it was so still and because the red roundabout, the green slide, and the blue swings were all grey in the moonlight. It looked like the ghost of a playground, or a faded clockwork toy waiting for daylight, and happy children to wind it up and set it going again. Linnet heard the town clock strike faintly. Midnight. She thought some of the moon silver must have got into the clock's works because it sounded softer, yet clearer than it did during the day. As she thought this she was startled to see shadows flicker over the face of the moon. 'Witches?' she wondered before she had time to tell herself that witches were only make-believe people. Of course it wasn't witches. It was a flock of birds flying inland from the sea.

'They're going to land on the river bank,' she thought. 'How funny, I didn't know birds could fly at night. I suppose it is because it is such bright moonlight.'

They landed and were lost to sight in a moment, but just as she began to look somewhere else a new movement caught her eye and she looked back again. Out from under the trees fringing the riverbank, from the very place where the birds had landed, came children running, bouncing and tumbling: their voices and laughter came to her, faint as chiming clock bells.

Linnet could see their bare feet shaking and crushing the grass, their wild floating hair, and even their mischievous shining eyes. They swarmed all over the playground. The swings began to swing, the seesaws started their up and down, the roundabout began to spin. The children laughed and played and frolicked while Linnet watched them, longing more than ever before to run out and join in the fun. It wasn't that she was afraid of the playground this time – it was just that she was shy. So she had to be content to stare while all the time the swings swept back and

forth loaded with the midnight children, and still more children crowded the roundabout, the seesaw and the bars.

How long she watched Linnet could not say. She fell asleep watching, and woke up with her cheek on the window-sill. The morning play-ground was quite empty and was bright in its daytime colours once more.

'Was it all dreams?' wondered Linnet blinking over breakfast. 'Will they come again tonight?'

'Wake up, stupid,' Alison called. 'It's time to be off. We'll be late for school.'

All day Linnet wondered about the playground and the children playing there by moonlight. She seemed slower and quieter than ever. Jim and Alison teased her calling her Old Dreamy, but Linnet did not tell them what dreams she had.

That night the moon woke Linnet once more and she sat up in a flash, peering out anxiously to

see if the midnight children were there. The playground, colourless and strange in its nightdress,
was empty, but within a minute Linnet heard
the beat of wings in the night. Yes, there were the
birds coming in from the sea, landing under the
trees and, almost at once, there were the children,
moonlit and laughing, running to the playground
for their night games. Linnet leaned farther out of
her window to watch them, and one of them
suddenly saw her and pointed at her. All the
children came and stood staring over the fence at
her. For a few seconds they just stayed like that,
Linnet peering out at them and the midnight
children, moonsilver and smiling, looking back at
her. Their hair, blown behind them by the wind,
was as pale as sea foam. Their eyes were as dark
and deep as sea caves and shone like stars.

Then the children began to beckon and wave
and jump up and down with their arms half out to
her, they began to skip and dance with delight.
Linnet slid out of bed, climbed out of the window
and over the fence all in her nightgown. The
midnight children crowded up to her, caught her
and whirled her away.

Linnet thought it was like dancing some
strange dance. At one moment she was on the
roundabout going round and round and giggling
with the other children at the prickly dizzy feeling
it gave her, in the next she was sweeping in a
follow-my-leader down the slide. Then someone
took her hand and she was on the seesaw with a

child before her and a child behind and three
more on the other end.

Up went the seesaw.

'Oh, I'm flying!' cried Linnet. Down went the

seesaw. Bump went Linnet, and she laughed at the unexpected bouncy jolt when the seesaw end hit the rubber tyre beneath it. Then she was on the swing. She had never been so high before. It seemed to Linnet that at any moment the swing was going to break free and fly off on its own, maybe to the land where the midnight children came from. The swing felt like a great black horse plunging through the night, like a tall ship tossing over the green waves.

'Oh,' cried Linnet, 'it's like having wings.' The children laughed with her, waved and smiled, and they swept around in their playground dance, but they didn't speak. Sometimes she heard them singing, but they were always too far away for her to hear the words.

When, suddenly, the midnight children left their games and started to run for the shadow of the trees, Linnet knew that for tonight at least she must go home as well, but she was too excited to feel sad. As she climbed through the window again she heard the beat of wings in the air and saw the birds flying back to the sea. She waved to them, but in the next moment they were quite gone, and she and the playground were alone again.

Next day when Alison and Jim set out for the playground Linnet said she was coming too. 'Don't come to me if you fall off anything,' said Jim scornfully.

Alison was kinder. 'I'll help you on the

roundabout,' she said. 'You hang on to me if you feel giddy.'

'But I won't feel giddy!' Linnet said, and Alison stared at her, surprised to hear her so confident and happy. However, this was just the beginning of the surprises for Alison and Jim. Linnet went on the roundabout and sat there without hanging on at all. On the swing she went almost as high as the boys, and she sat on the seesaw with her arms folded.

'Gosh, Linnet's getting brave as anything over at the playground,' said Jim at tea that night.

'I always knew she had it in her,' said Daddy.

The next night, and the next, Linnet climbed out of her window and joined the beckoning children in the silver playground. During the day, these midnight hours seemed like enchanted dreams and not very real. All the same Linnet was happy and excited knowing she had a special secret all to herself. Her eyes sparkled, she laughed a lot, and got braver and braver in the playground until all the children stopped what they were doing to watch her.

'Gee, Mum,' Alison said, 'you should see Linnet. She goes higher on the swing than any of the boys – much higher than Jim. Right up almost over the top.'

'I hope you're careful, dear,' her mother said.

'I'm all right,' Linnet cried. 'I'm not the least bit scared.'

'Linnet used to be frightened as anything,' Alison said, 'but now she's braver than anybody else.'

Linnet's heart swelled with pride. She could hardly wait until the moon and the tide brought her wonderful laughing night-time companions. She wanted them to admire her and gasp at her as the other children did. They came as they had on other nights, and she scrambled over the fence to join them.

'Look at me!' she shouted, standing on the end of the seesaw and going up and down. The child on the other end laughed and stood up too, but on its hands, not on its feet. It stayed there not over-balancing at all. Linnet slid away as soon as she could and ran over to the swings. She worked herself up higher and higher until she thought she was lost among the stars far far above the play-ground and the world, all on her own.

'Look at me,' she called again. 'Look at me.'

But the child on the next swing smiled over its shoulder and went higher – just a little higher. Then Linnet lost her temper.

'It's cleverer for me,' she shouted, 'because I'm a real live child, but you – you're only a flock of birds.'

Suddenly silence fell, the laughter died away, the singers stopped their songs. The swings swung lower, the roundabout turned slower, the seesaws stopped for a moment. Linnet saw all the children's pale faces turn towards her: then, without a sound, they began to run back to the shadow of the trees. Linnet felt cold with sadness. 'Don't go,' she called. 'Please don't go.' They did not seem to hear her.

'I'm sorry I said it,' she cried after them, her voice sounding very small and thin in the moonlit silent playground. 'I didn't mean it.' But no – they would not stop even though she pleaded, 'Don't go!' yet again. The playground was empty already and she knew she couldn't follow her midnight children. For the last time she spoke to them.

'I'm sorry!' she whispered and, although it was only a whisper, they must have heard because they answered her. Their voices and laughter drifted back happy and friendly saying their own goodbye. The next moment she saw for the last time the birds flying back over the sea to the secret land they came from. Linnet stood alone and barefooted in the playground, the wind pulling at her nightgown. How still and empty it was now. She pushed at a swing and it moved giving a sad little squeak that echoed all round. There was nothing for Linnet to do but go back to bed.

She was never afraid of the playground again and had lots and lots of happy days there laughing and chattering with her friends. Yet sometimes at night, when the moon rose and looked in at her window, she would wake up and look out at the playground just in case she should see the moon and the tide bringing her a flock of strange night-flying birds, which would turn into children and call her out to play with them. But the playground was always empty, the shining midnight children, with their songs and laughter, were gone for ever.

The Curiosity Concert

Down the street, watching and wondering, came Katie Stephenson, bringing her curiosity with her. She looked over hedges and through gateways. She looked up into trees and down into gutters.

Katie Stephenson was curious about everything – curious about streets, gardens and houses. Curious, mostly, about people and the different ways they lived and the different things they had around them. To Katie a simple walk to the shop was rather like a small circus. Every person she passed was doing some little act to entertain her. For instance, on the other side of the street Mrs Pope and Mrs Poole were walking together, wearing similar coats. But why was Mrs Pope wearing a big hat, and why was Mrs Poole carrying an umbrella on a perfectly fine day?

Mr J. G. Bingham – Katie knew his name, for it was on his yellow letter-box – was clipping his hedge and whistling softly to himself. Next door Mrs Floyd was smacking one of her twins. Katie watched to see if the other twin got smacked too, but Mrs Floyd marched back inside driving the bad twin before her.

Next door again was the Goodwin house.

Katie came to a full stop and peered closely down the slope of the lawn, hoping the door might open and she could look into Mrs Goodwin's hall and see Mrs Goodwin's new golden carpet. But the door stayed closed. The Goodwin house was so beautiful with its long green lawn and big trees and bright garden. Vines covered its veranda and there was a tennis court poking out from the back of the house. What could it be like inside? Katie wondered. Was everything soft and fluffy and golden like the carpet? Most houses she could guess at, but the wonderful Goodwin house was not a house that a girl with tangled hair and scratched knees could guess about very well.

When she came to the shop there was Mrs Goodwin herself buying a dozen eggs and some streaky bacon. She was wearing a beautiful white trouser-suit that made her shining hair look as golden as the new carpet. Katie stood as close to her as she could and sniffed at Mrs Goodwin's flowery smell. Mrs Goodwin did not notice Katie standing there, breathing deeply, staring at her as if she was learning her by heart.

'How's the boy?' asked Mr Gilbert the grocer.

'Oh, he's getting better all the time,' Mrs Goodwin replied. 'The doctor wants him in bed for three more days but – good heavens – he's sick of his room, his books, his games . . . nothing's right. I'm at my wit's end about keeping him amused, and he's so grumpy too.'

'Shows he's on the mend,' said Mr Gilbert cheerfully. 'And three days isn't so long.'

'Another three days and I'll be in bed beside him,' Mrs Goodwin sighed and walked out of the shop, flowery scent, shining hair and all, back to her beautiful house.

'Well, Katie – what can I do for you?' asked Mr Gilbert, but Katie was staring after Mrs Goodwin.

'Is it Jackie Goodwin you were talking about?'

'He's had rheumatic fever,' Mr Gilbert nodded. 'He'll have to take it quietly for a bit, I should think. It's tough on his Mum, though, because he's the sort of boy who thinks he owns the world at the best of times. I'll bet she's got her work cut out at present all right. What Jackie needs is a few brothers and sisters – no shortage of them down your way, eh Katie?'

Katie looked at Mr Gilbert for the first time. 'Mr Gilbert,' she said, 'you've given me an idea.'

In spite of her new golden carpet and her shining golden hair Mrs Goodwin was having a miserable day. Jackie wouldn't touch his scrambled eggs at lunch time.

Then he rubbed crayon into his blanket, almost, Mrs Goodwin thought, on purpose. And when she sat down to read to him a little later in the afternoon he wriggled and sighed until she stopped in the middle of the story and shut the book with a snap. Then Jackie cried.

'Oh, Jack!' said Mrs Goodwin, almost ready to cry herself.

At that very moment the front door bell rang. Mrs Goodwin went at once, but before she reached the door the bell rang again just as if somebody was trying it out, enjoying its soft chime. Mrs Goodwin opened the door. At first she thought the veranda was full of people. Then she saw that there were only five. Katie Stephenson was standing there and with her were her brothers Roddy and Tom and her two sisters, the bigger one Barbara holding the baby one, Catherine.

They were all dressed like people from fairy

stories. Katie wore a greeny-blue dress with a long train dragging behind it. On her head was a mask made to look like the head of a bird, with a yellow beak sticking out over her nose. Roddy was dressed as some sort of space man. He appeared to be covered almost entirely in cooking foil, and his face was painted green. Barbara, in a brown woolly jersey and tights, tail pinned on behind and a mask with a pointed nose, was probably meant to be a fox, but her brown eyes were soft and anxious, quite unfox-like, as they looked up at Mrs Goodwin. Thomas Stephenson was six – Jackie's own age – and he was dressed as a scarecrow with raggy clothes, a dreadful old hat and straw stuffed around his shoes, into his sleeves and down his neck, while the baby Catherine, in a long black dress and a hat like a black ice-cream cone, was the smallest witch Mrs Goodwin had ever seen.

'Oh, good heavens!' said Mrs Goodwin weakly.

'Good afternoon, Mrs Goodwin,' Katie Stephenson began. 'I was hearing in the shop today that Jackie wanted some entertainment. We are a concert party, Mrs Goodwin, come to put on a concert specially for Jackie. It's a good deed to visit the sick and my brother Roddy is a boy scout as well as a poet, so it can count as a good deed for him, as well as amusing Jackie.' She pointed to a black case behind her. 'I've brought my mother's piano accordion which I can play on

61

if you don't mind me being not absolutely perfect at it yet.'

Mrs Goodwin longed to tell them to go home but, even while she was thinking of kind words to say goodbye with, she thought of Jackie crying and cross in his room.

'Come on through,' she said, smiling suddenly. 'Jackie and I will really enjoy a concert. We're tired of everything else.'

The Stephensons stepped through on to her new golden carpet. Katie stared down and saw her school sandals pressing into the soft wool. She sniffed the smell of the Goodwins' house and lifted her eyes to snatch quick glimpses of pictures, a fish tank, and a grandfather clock with the sun and the moon on its face as well as all the usual numbers. At the same time Mrs Goodwin was snatching glances at the Stephensons.

'You've been to a lot of work,' she said. 'I like your costumes.'

'They're the fancy dresses we wore at the Christmas fancy dress party,' Barbara explained proudly. 'We don't get much chance to wear them.'

'I'm a peacock,' Katie said. 'Watch out for my tail, you kids.' She stared, enchanted, at a great vase of mixed flowers Mrs Goodwin had put upon her hall table only that morning.

'Jackie – you've got visitors,' Mrs Goodwin said, opening the door to Jackie's room. Jackie looked at them drearily from under cross red

eyelids. But then his eyes opened wider, his mouth lifted at the corners and he sat up on his crumpled pillows. Before he could say a word Katie began. She leaped into the space at the foot of his bed and cried:

'The Stephensons are here to present their famous variety concert – hours of laughter and song – something for everyone. Take your seat, madam,' she added to Mrs Goodwin; 'the curtain is up and the show is about to roll.' She bent over her black box. 'Give us a hand, Rod,' she muttered, hoisting out an old but well-polished piano accordion and struggling into the harness. At last she stood straight, her fingers on the yellowing keys. 'We will begin with a fine old song, "When father painted the parlour", sung by the famous Stephenson Harmonic Songsters.'

The Stephenson Harmonic Songsters began a

little shyly, but grew louder and more cheerful as the song progressed. Barbara had to put the baby Catherine down. She clung to Barbara's leg and danced by bending her knees and jigging up and down, without taking her feet off the floor. She sang too, but some song of her own that had nothing to do with father painting the parlour.

Mrs Goodwin clapped loudly and enthusiastically when the song was finished and Jackie joined in clapping and called, 'More, more!'

'And now the Stephensons will give the count-down and Roddy Stephenson will then give the actual, entire sound of a rocket taking off for Mars,' Katie announced. 'Come on, kids – ten, nine, eight, seven . . .'

The Stephensons all joined in, '. . . six, five, four, three, two, one, BLAST OFF!' they shouted. Roddy made the most remarkable sound ever heard in the Goodwin house – a kind of long shushing that slowly turned into a boom-ing roar. His face went red, his eyes screwed up and his shoulders hunched. It seemed hard to believe that anyone's throat could produce such a noise. When he finally ran out of breath, the noise stopped, his eyes opened, he saw Mrs Goodwin looking at him in astonishment, and he started to turn red again with embarrassment. Jackie was thrilled.

'Now Roddy will recite his famous space poem. Speak up, Roddy!'

Roddy, pleased with the applause his imitation of a rocket had won, began to recite rather shyly:

'Out of my ship between the stars
I stare out into space.
A thousand suns and galaxies
Look back into my face.

The suns are bright as trumpet calls,
The moons, like wind bells, chime.
I am the centre of a wheel
That spins in space and time.'

'There you are – pretty good, eh?' cried Katie. 'A poem which is going to be in the school magazine at the end of the year. Now Barbara will do a dance . . . a dance called "The Happy Fox".'

Katie's scratched fingers began to wander gently over the keys of the piano accordion, playing 'So early in the morning'. Barbara began to twirl and sweep the air with her arms. She ran to the right. She ran to the left. Her bushy tail bounced behind her. She pretended to catch some prey, tossing it into the air and catching it again. Katie watched her proudly and played a few wrong notes. At last Barbara's dance was over. Then Katie picked up Catherine and held her cleverly with her right arm while, with her left hand, she pushed Thomas the scarecrow forward.

'Now the poem of "The Witch and the

Scarecrow",' she announced. 'I'm saying this one, because it is my favourite:

> 'Out in the fields of tossing grass
> A scarecrow saw a witch go past.
> Her hair was pale as thistledown
> Her tall hat had a pointed crown.
>
> Her face was full of magic wild
> She was a witch's magic child
> And, softly, as she went along
> She sang a strange enchanted song.
>
> The scarecrow could not say a word
> Of what he'd seen and what he'd heard,
> He stood all day the corn amid
> And kept the witch's secret hid.'

Katie did not look at Mrs Goodwin or Jackie while she said her poem. She looked over their heads and seemed to see, somewhere behind them on Jackie's white wall, the shadows of the scarecrow and the witch in their grassy fields. Really she was looking at Jackie's animal posters, and the clown puppet that hung from a hook in the corner.

'That poem,' she went on, 'was written by Roddy Stephenson, and was in last year's school magazine. And now,' she said, as Mrs Goodwin and Jackie clapped cheerfully, 'there will be a few minutes while the Stephensons get their breaths again. After that the show will continue. Peppermints will be served all round at half-time.'

'I'll just go out into the kitchen for a moment,' Mrs Goodwin said. 'Call me when the concert is about to go on again.'

What with showing Jackie how to play the piano accordion, and what with Jackie showing Tom how to work the clown puppet, the half-time was rather long. Before the concert had started again Mrs Goodwin came back into the room with tea. She had made delicious white toast and covered it with scrambled egg, grated cheese and thin strips of bacon all grilled to a sizzling brown. There were slices of date square and fruitcake and glasses with orange juice and ice and a coloured straw in each glass. It was a regular party being held in Jackie's room.

'Oh boy,' cried Roddy. 'I haven't seen such a tea since Mum got her job.'

'Or even before,' said Katie. 'Mum doesn't do much cooking, not the cake sort of cooking. She's good on spaghetti, but not so good on cakes.'

'She doesn't like sewing much either,' said Barbara.

Jackie looked interested. 'What does she like doing?' he asked.

'She likes poetry and dancing,' said Tom. 'She can sing and play the guitar and the piano accordion.'

'She likes to go on picnics,' said Barbara.

'Last time Mum made a cake we took it on a

picnic and had it for pudding. We called it Picnic Pudding Cake,' Roddy added, taking another slice of date square.

'I wish I had some of that cake,' Jackie remarked wistfully. Then he ate toast covered with cheese, bacon and the scrambled eggs he had refused for lunch.

After the refreshments the concert continued. The first item was Tom, standing on his head, dropping straw everywhere, and singing 'What shall we do with a drunken sailor?' The second item was riddles, which Mrs Goodwin and Jackie had to answer because the Stephensons knew the answers already. The third item was a dance. Katie played 'Hands, Knees and Boomps-a-daisy'

on the piano accordion. Roddy danced with Barbara and Tom tried to dance with Catherine. But after a little while Mrs Goodwin got up and danced with Tom because Catherine preferred to do a little jumping dance of her own. Jackie longed to join in.

'Next week, Jackie. Next week!' called Katie cheerfully.

To finish the concert she played 'Waltzing Matilda', which was the tune she knew best, and everyone, even Jackie, was able to join in on this last item.

'And now,' cried Katie, her voice sounding rather hoarse, 'the Stephenson concert party is over. The Stephensons have to go home and put the vegetables on. But don't worry, friends — they'll be back.'

'Will you really?' Jackie demanded. 'Will you be back tomorrow?'

'Do come!' Mrs Goodwin said, and you could see that she meant it. 'It's been wonderful for Jackie, and I've enjoyed the concert too.'

Katie looked uncertain. Then she smiled. 'Oh, we'll probably be able to drop in,' she replied in a lordly fashion. 'The show must go on.'

The Stephensons left Jackie and his mother much more cheerful than they had found them.

As they went along Barbara said, 'That was a good idea of yours, Katie. It's fun doing good deeds.'

'Don't take too much notice of her good-deed

talk,' replied Roddy, looking sternly at Katie. 'It was just an excuse to get into the Goodwin house. She's been mad with curiosity about that house for months and months.'

'So what!' Katie said, turning up her nose. 'I *like* being curious.'

Telephone Detectives

As he dug among the tough, spreading roots in the bamboo corner, Monty heard something clink against the spade. A moment later he turned up a little black metal box – treasure! – something he had often dreamed of finding. He knew it was treasure, and it crossed his mind that it was funny that he should find treasure this day of all days.

Today was the day of the school picnic. The children of Deepford, in New Zealand, were going over the hills to the beach, for swimming, sandwiches, cakes, lemonade – and a treasure hunt. All the children had gone, except Monty. Monty had watched the buses and the cars go by for a while, and then he had gone round to the back fence because he just could not bear it any longer. He had sat down among the bamboos in the bamboo corner and felt sad, in a hot and angry kind of way.

Monty had chicken-pox. There were a few spots on his face, but mostly they were under his shirt, all itching away like mad. Monty wished he felt really sick, then he wouldn't want to go to a picnic. As it was, apart from the itches, he felt quite well and full of longings – especially for the treasure hunt. Nothing seemed fair. In a horrid

way he enjoyed feeling miserable and being angry at the other children who didn't have chicken-pox. He lay on the warm ground under the bamboos and sulked.

But that was a while ago now, for Monty's thoughts had slowly changed. First he had started thinking that the day was beautiful. Then he had noticed a bird hopping on the lawn. A spider swung on its thread, and a tiny little atom of a grub looped itself madly up a thick bamboo stem. 'All those things are going on,' thought Monty, 'and none of them knows or cares that I'm here feeling sad . . .'

The sight of all these tiny restless creatures, all doing something, had made Monty feel better. He had decided to clean out the bamboo corner for his mother, who was really sorry that he had chicken-pox and couldn't go to the school picnic. It was a plan that he could always change if he found he wasn't enjoying it . . .

So that was how Monty came to find the little black box. He picked it up. It was dirty and rusted round the hinges, but that only made it look older and all the more interesting. Monty sat down on the grass and worked round the lid of the box with a stick until he had loosened it a little.

Then he ran to the workshop and found the oil-can. He worked oil all round the hinges and round the edges where he had loosened the rust. At last he felt the lid really move and, after trying again, he wriggled it off. The box was open.

Inside were four lovely big marbles with twisty nets of colour winding through their glass. There was a bear carved out of wood, and a little pocket-knife with a handle that might be made of silver. There was a bit of blue glass worn smooth by the sea and filled with watery sea lights. Last of all there was a necklace . . . a pattern of greeny-blue stones hung on a delicate, dull chain. Monty touched it carefully, and wondered.

He decided to take it to his father.

'Treasure, treasure!' he shouted, running round the house and into the kitchen where his parents were having a quiet cup of tea.

'What have you got there?' his father said, taking up the little box and peering into it curiously. His expression changed as he saw the necklace and as Monty told his story.

'If it wasn't for the necklace, we needn't worry,' his father said at last. 'But I think it's probably rather valuable. It looks like turquoise, to me . . . turquoises on a silver chain. How on earth did it get there?'

'If we were detectives,' Monty said, 'we could find out. We could go to the people who lived in this house before us, and ask . . . But we aren't detectives, and I've got chicken-pox.'

His father suddenly laughed. 'What's the phone for, Monty? It might have been invented just for detectives with chicken-pox. I'll start! I'll ring up Mr Davis. We bought the house from him, and he might be able to tell us something.'

Monty waited by the phone as his father rang. He tried to guess from his father's words what Mr Davis was saying. It was nothing interesting. Mr Davis knew nothing about boxes of treasure buried in the garden.

Monty's father put down the phone. 'He says that the people who lived here while he was letting the house, before we bought it, had only grown-up daughters.'

'It's a boy's treasure,' said Monty. 'All but the necklace.'

'I think you're right. Anyway, that family moved down to Victoria. Mr Davis bought the house from a Miss Dunbar. She's dead now,' said Monty's father, frowning.

'Her sisters are alive, though,' said Mother unexpectedly. 'Mrs Casely at the Milk Bar is one of them – she might be able to tell us something. She'll be at work this morning.'

'Your turn to phone!' said his father, holding out the phone to Mother. 'Anyway, you know this Mrs Casely.'

Mrs Casely had a booming voice, and Monty could hear it clearly when his mother rang, coming all the way over the wires from the Milk Bar where she had worked for years.

'Turquoises?' she bellowed. 'No, no, nothing like that! No! She had some nice pearls once – well, not real ones, you know, but nice – you couldn't tell the difference. But not turquoises! Well, I don't know! We were there from childhood. Maybe if you were to ring Mr Mills – Horatio Mills, that is – he's still alive. He had the house before my father bought it. He's been around since the year dot.'

'What does she mean – the year dot?' asked Monty when his mother had put down the phone.

'She means he's lived around here for a long time,' said his father. 'Listen, Monty, it's your turn to ring. Why should we do all your dectective work for you? Let's see, now ... Mills, H. D. Here's the number. He lives over at Carden now, it seems.'

Monty took the phone firmly and dialled the

number. He heard the distant phone bell going
brrr . . . brrr . . . brrr . . . then a gentle old voice
spoke suddenly in his ear. 'Hallo?'

'Is that Mr Horatio Mills?' Monty asked.

'Yes!' said the voice, sounding grave and
rustly.

Monty told him who he was and where he
lived, and explained that they were trying to
locate people who had once lived in the house
because of something they had found.

'What sort of thing?' asked Mr Horatio Mills.

'It's something I dug up,' said Monty cautiously.

'Indeed!' said Mr Mills. 'Not a little metal box
with marbles in it?'

'And a knife!' said Monty.

76

'And a turquoise necklace!' said Mr Horatio Mills.

His voice sounded quite firm and brisk all at once. 'I'll come across right away.'

'You'd better not,' said Monty sadly. 'Not unless you've had chicken-pox, which is what I've got.'

There was a strange sound over the phone: it seemed that Mr Horatio Mills might be laughing.

'I have had it,' he said. 'Indeed . . . but I'll tell you about that when I see you. I'll drive over now.'

It took twenty minutes for Mr Horatio Mills to arrive. He drove up in an old car, very clean and shining. Mr Horatio Mills was rather like his car – very old, but very spruce and well cared for.

He smiled at Monty's parents, and shook hands with Monty. 'Mr Monty Forest, I presume?' he said.

Monty nodded. He felt too excited to speak.

The box was on the table. Mr Horatio Mills got out his glasses, polished them and put them on. He examined the box and touched it with his thin old hands. 'Yes . . .' he said at last. 'This is the box.' He picked up the little pocket knife. 'This was mine, once.'

'I can see it's a most exciting story,' said Mother. 'Let me pour you a cup of tea, and you can tell us all about Monty's find.' She settled old Mr Mills in a sunny chair with a cup of tea before he was allowed to begin his story.

'My father built this house,' he began. 'At that time there were no other houses on this ridge. It stood in the middle of fields and trees. There was a big tree where the garage is now, and a long garden stretching down the slope. My brothers and I played in that big tree a lot. Our favourite game was pirates. We swarmed up and down its branches like a troop of monkeys, pretending we were reefing sails and climbing up the rigging. There were three of us – Thomas, Reginald and Horatio – that's me.

'One day Thomas, who was the eldest and made all the plans, decided that he would bury a treasure, and we must find it, we younger ones. We all had to put something into the box, but when we had done this it still looked rather empty, so Thomas did a very naughty thing. He sneaked upstairs to our mother's room and pirated one of her necklaces. It made it seem much more like real pirate treasure, I must admit. Then off he went and hid the box . . . but, as you see, we didn't find it.'

'But Thomas would remember where he'd put it,' said Monty, puzzled. 'Even if you and Reginald couldn't find it – he'd know where it was.'

'That's just it!' said Mr Horatio Mills, quite enjoying himself. 'He *didn't* remember. We began our search by climbing up the big tree. We thought he might have hidden it there. Thomas climbed up with us – and he slipped, and fell. He

had what is called concussion. We were all very
worried about him for a day or two, but he got
better after that. The only thing was ... he
couldn't remember one single thing about the day
of his accident. So we just didn't know where he
had hidden the treasure, and though we searched
and searched, we never found it.'

'It was in the bamboo corner under the fence,'
Monty said.

'So!' said Mr Horatio Mills, and nodded his
head. 'The bamboo had just been planted then.
And you must remember there was a lot more

land and garden to search in those days. How funny that another boy should have found it after all these years! I'll take the necklace back for my little grand-daughter, if you don't mind, but I'd like you to have the rest of the treasure, Monty. It isn't a very valuable or exciting treasure, but it is truly old, and it was truly buried and lost.'

Monty drew a deep breath. 'I think it's a wonderful treasure,' he said. 'It seems special somehow, because there were boys who buried it all those years ago – just the same sort of treasure I might bury myself, if I had to.' He looked round at his mother and father, then back to Mr Horatio Mills. 'And it seems funny to think I was sad at missing the school treasure hunt today – and then found another treasure here, all through having chicken-pox! Golly, Mr Mills, I hope you don't catch it!'

Mr Mills smiled. 'I don't expect I will. I've already had it. In fact' – and his eyes twinkled behind his glasses – 'it was because Thomas, Reginald and I had chicken-pox that we were at home that sunny day all those years ago when Thomas buried the treasure!'

The Letter

There was once a boy called James who lived with his father and grandmother in a flat in the city. His grandmother said the flat was 'convenient', and by this she meant it was close to James's father's office, close to the shops in the city's main street, and close to the school as well. Indeed the school was just across the road, but James did not find it convenient at all. All his friends lived miles away and came to school in buses, and of course this meant that they lived miles away from James too, so that in the holidays, when there was no school, he was often very lonely.

His grandmother did her best. She played snakes and ladders with him and helped him make wonderful scrap books. She spread newspaper out on the carpet so that he could paint, and read him all sorts of exciting stories. In spite of all this, James used to miss the company of boys, and he would feel lonely for all sorts of things he had never really done before – lonely for going barefoot, climbing trees, shouting, fighting and catching frogs. Quite a lot of people have felt like this at one time or another when they were eight years old, but James did something about it, and it happened like this.

Every now and then at dinner time Mr Wilson, James's father, would stare into space for a moment and then say, 'I wonder how Dorian Ashley is getting on these days.'

Then Mrs Wilson, James's grandmother, would look disapproving, but James would prick up his ears, waiting for his father to go on.

Mr Wilson would start dreamily, 'Do you re-

member one time when Dorian Ashley . . .' and then would come a story. From listening to all these 'Do you remembers . . .' James learnt enough stories about Dorian Ashley to fill a book as long as a scrap book and many times as thick.

Dorian Ashley had been a great one for running away from places. First he had run away from school, and then he ran away from home and went to sea. Then he ran away to get married, and when he was married, he and his wife went all over the world having strange adventures. Dorian Ashley had flown aeroplanes, got shipwrecked on an island, had ridden elephants and camels. He had hunted man-eating tigers, and had worked in a circus wrestling a bear. The stories went on and on and there appeared to be no end to the things he had done.

Dorian Ashley soon seemed like some hero, vast and shadowy, with his feet in the forests and his head blotting out the moon, striding around the world from island to island. What was most surprising of all was that this mysterious wild man wasn't just a person in an adventure book, but was actually James's uncle, and the wife he had run away with was James's aunt. They had some children too, but neither Mr nor Mrs Wilson knew very much about them, which was a pity. James used to wonder about them, for they were his cousins and he felt he wanted to know them, more than he wanted anything else in the world.

Then one day his father cleared out a forgotten box and gave James a few big envelopes, some spare paper, an old diary with blank pages for drawing in and a few other things. Looking through the diary James found an address staring up at him. It was written in big sprawling writing and it said, 'Dorian Ashley, Hill House, Titirangi, Auckland, New Zealand.'

So that was where Uncle Dorian lived, thought James. An idea came to him. He would write a letter to his uncle and aunt and cousins and post it without telling anyone. How surprised his father and grandmother would be when he showed them the letter he would get in reply!

So that is what James did. He wrote as carefully and neatly as he could. First he told his uncle and aunt and cousins who he was. Then he told them how well he was feeling and what class he was in at school. After this he told them how very much he would like to meet them, and what fine weather it was in Wellington at present, and then he felt he had written quite enough. After all he was only eight and found writing quite hard work. He put the letter in one of the big brown envelopes his father had given him, bought a stamp with his own money, and posted it.

James waited and waited for letters, but not one came. At first he felt all warm and excited inside and then, later, he felt sad, but no matter how he felt there was no answer at all. At last he told his father what he had done, but his father

just smiled and said, 'Uncle Dorian left that place years and years ago and we haven't heard from him since. What a pity! He would have written to you if he had been there. He liked children very much and would have been pleased to get a letter from you.'

As time went by James forgot about the letter though not about his Uncle Dorian and unknown cousins. However, there was a surprise in store for him and a year later, when he was nine and it was school holidays again, the surprise happened.

There he was sitting at dinner with his grandmother and father, feeling that the holidays were going to be just a little dull and uninteresting, when there was a *click* out in the hall. Someone had opened the front door without knocking. His father and grandmother looked at each other in surprise as footsteps came swiftly towards the dining-room. Then, as they all watched, amazed, the dining-room door slowly opened, and someone James had never seen before came in.

He was a huge man so untidily dressed that he looked like a giant scarecrow. His hair which was copper-coloured came down almost to his collar, and his eyes burned greenish-blue under their coppery brows, in a face which was a deep hard brown with sun and wind.

They all stared at one another for a moment.

'Goodness gracious! It's Dorian!' said Mr Wilson. He sounded delighted.

'Dorian!' said Grandmother Wilson. She sounded disapproving, but then James could see at a glance that this was the sort of uncle his grandmother would disapprove of, especially in her clean convenient house.

'What on earth are you doing here, Dorian?' she asked.

'I was invited,' said Uncle Dorian, smiling a slow warm smile.

'Not by me!' said Grandmother Wilson firmly.

Then Uncle Dorian took from his pocket a folded, crumpled, dirty brown envelope. It was crissed and crossed all over in different sorts of writing – square writing, pointed writing, writing with loops and plain writing. Different languages jostled each other from top to bottom on both sides. But the largest squarest letters were printed on the front in James's own faded printing.

'Mr Dorian Ashley,' they said. It was James's own letter to his uncle, readdressed and re-stamped many times.

'James sent it to me,' Uncle Dorian said. His voice was dark and rough-sounding, as if it was a black bear speaking and not a man. 'This letter has chased me all round the world. It has gone through France, Egypt, Hong Kong, South America . . . friends of mine kept on sending it on by plane, train and by sea too. It's a widely travelled letter and I think I'll keep it for ever. Funnily enough it had to come all the way back home to find me. I came to see James and to invite him to come up north with me and spend the holidays with his cousins – but since I'm here and I've got a lot of room in the car, why don't you all pack up and come? You'd all be welcome.'

And that is just what they did. Mr Wilson took a special holiday from the office and off they went to Uncle Dorian's house by the sea, and had the most exciting holiday you could imagine. James found he had five cousins, some older than he was, and some younger. One of them, however, was a boy just his own age. When the weather was fine, they taught him how to swim, how to make houses in trees and dams over the creek. When it rained James showed them how to make scrap books, and little dishes and animals out of clay, which they painted and baked in the oven.

So everybody was happy, and learning something new. Even Grandmother Wilson forgot to look disapproving and enjoyed the sun and sand. She got quite brown.

Every holiday after that James went to stay with his cousins (for, after all his travelling, Uncle Dorian had settled down to write a book about his adventures), so James was never lonely in the holidays again.

But, mind you, this would never have happened if James hadn't written that letter which had chased Uncle Dorian round the world, reminding him at last that he had a nephew in Wellington. The letter couldn't tell of its adventures but no doubt it had had some. It certainly looked adventurous in its battered way, like an old pirate with memories of strange ports and people, and whenever it was shown to anybody the different writings and languages on it spoke to them in the voices of the world.

The Girl Who Loved Cars

Roberta, who was usually called Bobby, lived on a sheep station in the High Country of New Zealand. She was far from shops and schools and other girls, but she wasn't lonely because of her family, the animals, the very mountains themselves and the cars. Her family was her father and mother and her four big brothers. Because there were five men in the family, all wanting to go to different places at different times, and because farms use a lot of machinery, the backyard of

Bobby's farmhouse was filled with machines of one kind or another – tractors, motor bikes, but mostly cars. So, from the time she was very small, Bobby had learned about engines.

The cars were all her friends. 'Mademoiselle Fifi Le Bonbon' was the full name of the Citroën Safari, but it was usually called Fifi. 'Gretchen' was the name of the Volkswagen. 'The Bitzer' was a car her brother Michael had put together himself, and then there was the old Model T Ford which had been in the family for years, and could only go east because the mountains in the west were rather too much for its aged engine. This car was known as 'Nancy', 'Old Nance' or 'Rattling Nan', as well as a number of other fiercer names, depending upon how she was going.

Bobby knew all these cars well. Whenever their bonnets were open she was there, peering in, asking questions and listening to all the car talk going on over her head.

She longed for the day when she would have a car of her own to drive. As she passed the spanners and oily rags she dreamed of tuning motors herself and making them purr like happy cats.

Because she herself was so far away from any town Bobby could not go to school in the ordinary fashion. She was a member of the Correspondence School. Her lessons arrived for her weekly, in big green plastic envelopes, and her teachers spoke to her over the radio at half past nine every morning. Bobby worked hard and listened hard, and yet, always, over the voices on the radio she could hear the voices of the cars in her own yard telling her who was going out and where they were going. Every engine spoke with the voice of a friend. She even heard a voice from the sky at times, when a cropduster was flying overhead with fertilizer for the barren land farther to the west.

Though she enjoyed belonging to the Correspondence School, naturally Bobby wondered from time to time just what it was like to go to school with other children.

'. . . to a real school,' said Karen Williams, pretty, fair Karen who sometimes came with her parents to visit Bobby's family.

'The Correspondence School is a real school too,' Bobby replied. 'It's just that we are all spread around, and aren't all together in the same room.'

'Part of school is being in the same room,' Karen said. 'It's not all lessons. It's playing too, and talking.'

'Well, it sounds fun,' Bobby said with a thoughtful sigh, 'but I just can't go to a school like that, not yet anyway.'

One Saturday, when Karen and her parents came visiting, Bobby had some news.

'Next week I'm going to school for a day,' she said. 'It's all arranged. Mum's going to town in Fifi and I'm going with her. I'm going to spend the day at school while Mum's shopping and visiting.'

'That's good,' Karen said with her warm, slow smile. Then she chuckled. 'You'll have to be careful, though, Bobby, or they'll sit you with the boys. I bet they think you're a boy.'

'But I've got long hair,' Bobby said, a little indignantly.

'So have a lot of boys!' Karen replied. 'And you talk about cars all the time. Only boys talk about cars.'

Bobby was surprised. She had thought that girls talked about cars too.

'It's useful to know,' she argued. 'Cars are important. There's a lot of money wrapped up in cars.'

Karen laughed again. 'Cars are important,' she agreed, 'but it's men who know about cars. Girls mostly know about sewing and cooking and things like that . . . house things, not car things. No one expects a girl to know about cars.'

After that they did not say any more about cars, for the wind from the south-east began to have rain in it. They ran inside and spent the rest of Karen's visit doing jigsaw puzzles while the wind and the rain lashed and beat outside.

Karen and her parents had to leave quite early, for it was a long drive home. Luckily, just before they left, the rain clouds rolled away carrying the fierce storm with them.

Bobby decided to walk up Petticoat Hill. It was

her own special hill because she had given it its name when she was very small. She had looked out of her window one June morning and had seen thin snow covering the hill, with tufts of tussock breaking through, wild and golden.

'The hill is wearing its petticoat,' Bobby had cried, because she had a petticoat that she loved, a white petticoat sprigged with golden flowers.

There was no snow now, though the ground was so wet that if you listened you could hear the prickling sound of water soaking into the earth. The tussocks tossed like horses' manes, splashing Bobby with beads of water as they quarrelled with the wind. Bobby trudged uphill, her hands in her pockets, thinking about school, and cars, and being a girl.

Would people think she was a boy? She was always quite pleased when she was called a tomboy. But what if people began to think you were a boy, didn't know you for what you really were . . . Bobby thought she would not like that. She began to feel worried and ill at ease. Would she have to go by that stiff name 'Roberta' just to show she was a girl? If she called herself Bobby, it would only make matters worse, for Bobby was a boy's name as often as not. Suddenly Bobby thought she did not want to go to school on Tuesday week. She just wanted to stay where she was, where everyone knew who she was and what she was.

Instead of going to the very top of Petticoat Hill she decided to go to the right, slide down on to the road and go back to the farmhouse that way. Scrambling down the bank on to the road she was startled to find she was not alone. A young woman, with reddish-brown hair and wearing a smart grey trouser-suit, was walking down the rough road looking uncertainly at the puddles on either side. Few cars came this way, for there were gates to open and shut, and the road itself was muddy in the winter and dusty in the summer. At least the rain had laid the dust, thought Bobby, staring, too shy to speak first.

'Hello,' the young woman said. 'Do you live near here? My car won't go. I was driving along quite smoothly and suddenly the engine stopped for no reason that I could see.'

'Cut out on you, did it?' Bobby's voice was puzzled and thoughtful. 'What sort of car are you driving?'

'A Mini,' the woman replied a little impatiently. 'I've just got to get home somehow. I just can't let myself get stuck up here a thousand miles from anywhere.'

'Was it raining when the engine cut out?' Bobby asked.

'Pelting down!' the woman said, pulling a face. 'I felt as if I was shipwrecked sitting there in that little car with the rain streaming down all around.'

'I bet I know what's wrong. I bet you've

got water in your distributor,' Bobby said confidently.

'Well, what had I better do?' the woman asked. 'Is it serious?'

'It could be all right already,' Bobby answered. 'It'll dry out on its own . . . unless you kept on trying to start it and flattened the battery. Then it might take longer.' The woman looked guilty. 'Did you?' said Bobby accusingly.

'I might have . . . a bit,' the woman answered.

'We'd better take a look,' Bobby said. 'It's just up over the rise, is it? Otherwise you could have let it roll on down.'

Together they trudged up the road with the wind pushing behind them.

The car was in a little dip just over the shoulder of Petticoat Hill. It was almost new and a bright shiny red.

'It's pretty,' said Bobby politely, though her favourite colour was a dark green . . . British

Racing Green. 'Ladybird would be a good name for your car. Has it got a name?'

'Not really,' said the woman, looking rather surprised.

'All our cars have names,' Bobby explained, and opened the bonnet of the little red car. Timothy had had a very similar car at home last Christmas that he was taking care of for a friend holidaying in Australia. She had driven in it with Timothy and he had told her quite a lot about it. If the woman had only known it, Bobby was re-membering Timothy and copying his words and tone of voice. Now Bobby peered down at the distributor.

'Stone the flipping crows!' she hissed. 'Just look at that. Wet as a trout! Of course the wind wouldn't help, it would just blow the rain straight in through the grill.' She turned to the woman. 'Hop into the car, will you, and just try to turn the motor over.'

The car coughed hopefully but did not start.

'Have you got a soft cloth in there?' Bobby asked, and looked rather dubiously at the yellow duster the woman handed her. 'We can but try,' said Bobby, which was a phrase often used by her brother Philip. She began to dry carefully round the distributor.

The next time the woman tried to start her car the engine cleared its throat and then came alive, rumbling gently to itself. Bobby felt successful and grinned happily as she let the bonnet fall.

'You're a wonder!' the woman said, smiling too. 'I've never met a girl who knew so much about cars.'

Bobby suddenly looked gloomy. She stopped feeling as if her brothers were with her reminding her what to do. She remembered school and felt alone.

'Oh well,' she muttered, 'it's not much good in some ways. It only makes people think you must be a boy.'

'A boy!' exclaimed the woman scornfully. 'No one would ever think you were a boy. You look just like a girl, but you're clever enough to know something extra. I'm extremely grateful to you. I could have walked for miles and not found such good help.'

'It's downhill for quite a long way from here,' Bobby said. 'You should be all right. It will probably keep on keeping on now. If it cuts out again, put her into neutral and coast down for a bit – then, when she gets a bit of speed on, change into second – or third –' For the first time Bobby looked uncertain. She secretly crossed her fingers and said: '. . . into second, say . . .'

'I'll try to remember,' the woman said, 'and listen, I'll call my car Ladybird as you suggested, in memory of our meeting.'

The car rolled forward and down the hill. Bobby watched it until it was out of sight, until it was as tiny as a real ladybird. Then she scrambled up the hill and went home grinning to herself all the way.

'That was fun,' she thought. 'I'm sorry it's over.'

But some things don't end as easily as that.

When Bobby's mother drove up to the school on Tuesday week a familiar car was parked next to the bicycle shed in the playground.

'Bobby, this is Miss Clark,' said Bobby's mother a few moments later, introducing Bobby to her new teacher for a day. Bobby looked at the reddish brown hair and the smart grey trouser-suit.

'I knew it was you,' she said. 'I saw your Ladybird outside.'

'Oh, my rescuer!' cried Miss Clark. 'What a small world!'

'Put it on four wheels it is,' Bobby said, quoting her brother Gerard.

'Don't start the machinery talk, Bobby,' her mother began, but Miss Clark laughed and shook her head.

'It's a joke between Bobby and me,' she said. 'We're old friends.'

She sat Bobby at a real school desk and told the children all about the Correspondence School and Bobby's beautiful lonely land up in the High Country with the sheep and the tussock.

'And remember, children,' she went on, 'how I told you about my car stopping, the weekend before last, up in the High Country? Remember how I told you about the young rescuer who came out of the tussock and helped me? We did not tell each other our names but when I met Bobby this morning I recognized her at once, looking like a regular schoolgirl.'

Bobby was shy but pleased, and though she felt a bit silly at being called a rescuer she knew Miss Clark meant it in a kindly way.

Later in the afternoon she wrote an essay with the other school children all about what she wanted to do when she grew up.

This is what Bobby wrote:

'What I want to do most is a very hard thing. I want to drive in a Formula One Grand Prix. I'm not very much worried about winning, though I would try hard to win. What I want is to drive really fast without any fear of getting a ticket, for you have to pay three dollars for every mile you are doing over the limit. I want to drive fast and feel the car working perfectly, all its systems fitting in together. I am starting to practise for this now in my thoughts. My mother says it is ridiculous but my father says, "There is a first time for everything and why not?"'

And when Miss Clark read Bobby's essay, she laughed her deep laugh and said 'And why not?' too.

The Tick-Tock Party

One day Timothy said to his mother, 'It is a long time since Christmas came. We haven't had a party for a long time. Will it be my birthday soon?'

'Not for another long time!' his mother said. 'We are half-way between Christmas time and birthday time.'

'Couldn't we have my birthday a bit sooner this year?' asked Timothy.

'Not really!' said his mother. 'It is best to have your birthday when it comes.'

Timothy looked around sadly. Out in the yard he saw Tick-Tock the old grey rocking-horse.

'Couldn't it be Tick-Tock's birthday then?' he asked. 'Tick-Tock is so old his birthday cake would be like a bonfire with all its candles. Let it be his birthday.'

Mother thought for a while.

'Yes,' she said, 'Tick-Tock deserves a birthday. He is very old indeed. First he was Granny's rocking-horse, then he was mine. Now he is yours. His mane has come off and his tail is lost. All his fine paint is gone. He must feel very old and grey. We will have a party on Saturday to cheer him up.'

Timothy ran out into the yard to tell Tick-Tock.

'It is your birthday on Saturday, Tick-Tock,' he said. 'Isn't that exciting? Aren't you pleased?'

But Tick-Tock just looked as sad and grey as ever. Timothy was the one to be excited. Thursday went by, and then Friday. At last it was Saturday – the day of the birthday. It was a beautiful sunny morning. Timothy woke up and the first thing he did was to run outside, pyjamas and all, to say 'Happy Birthday' to Tick-Tock. He ran into the sunny yard, and stopped in surprise. Tick-Tock was not grey any more. He was shining white all over.

Mother and Father laughed at Timothy's surprise. 'This is part of my birthday present to Tick-Tock,' Father said. 'I will give him the rest of his present this afternoon when the white paint is quite dry.'

Timothy was very pleased to think that Tick-Tock had got a birthday present.

All morning he played in the yard. He could not keep his eyes off the shining white shape of Tick-Tock.

Just before lunch a car pulled up at the gate.

'Mummy!' called Timothy. 'Here are Granny and Grandpa!'

'We couldn't miss Tick-Tock's birthday,' Granny said. 'I have a present for him.'

Tick-Tock couldn't unwrap his present, so Timothy had to unwrap it for him. Granny had made a fine red saddle with golden tassels. Grandpa had a parcel too. At first Timothy could not think what it was. It seemed to be filled with long black hair.

'It is a new tail for Tick-Tock made of real horse-hair,' said Grandpa. 'Your father will nail it on for him – and the saddle too – when the paint is dry.'

So now Tick-Tock had a new white coat, a red saddle and a black tail.

Someone opened the gate. It was Aunty Joan.

'I had to come to Tick-Tock's party,' she said. 'Here is his present.'

Timothy unwrapped the parcel. It was full of brown sheep's wool.

'It is from a special brown sheep I know,' said Aunty Joan. 'It is a mane for Tick-Tock, but I see you will have to wait before we put it on.'

So now Tick-Tock had a fine brown mane to toss in the wind.

'It does not match his tail,' said Timothy, 'but that is all the better.'

Then Anne, Timothy's big sister, came out of her bedroom.

'Look,' she said, 'I have a present for Tick-Tock too. It is a red bridle. I made it all myself.'

'Thank you,' said Timothy, because Tick-Tock was too busy thinking about his presents to say 'thank you' for himself.

'Well, this is all very well,' said Timothy's mother, 'but *my* present to Tick-Tock is waiting inside. Let's go in and look at it.'

Inside, the table was set for lunch, and in the middle of the table was a big birthday cake with more candles on it than Timothy had ever seen. Everyone laughed and talked and ate birthday cake.

It was a wonderful party. Outside Tick-Tock stood like a ghost horse, white and shining in the sunlight.

'Ah,' said Granny, 'I remember the morning when I first saw Tick-Tock. It was Christmas, and I was only a little girl then. He was the most wonderful Christmas present I had ever had. He was dapple grey in those days with a long white mane and tail.'

'Then, when I was small,' said Aunty Joan, 'Father – that's Grandpa to you Timothy – brought him down from the loft and painted him up again.'

'Aunty Joan and I used to play on him for hours at a time,' said Mother. 'We'd ride him together, or pretend he was a wild horse we were trying to catch and tame. Whenever I felt sad I would go and sit on Tick-Tock and rock and rock until I felt better.'

'And now he's mine,' said Timothy proudly.

'Quite a member of the family in fact,' said Father. 'I think the paint is dry enough now. We'll give Tick-Tock a really new look for his birthday.'

They all went out and watched Father nail on the black tail and tack on the brown mane. He fitted the saddle and bridle on and fastened them with little nails. Last of all he took a pot of blue paint, and with a small paint brush he painted two beautiful blue eyes for Tick-Tock to see with.

'Good old Tick-Tock,' said Anne. 'He looks like new.'

'He's smiling at me,' Timothy cried.

'So he should be, with all those presents,' said Father, laughing. He lifted Timothy on to the new red saddle. 'You give him a birthday present now, Timothy,' Father said. 'Take him for a good rocky ride.'

So Timothy rocked away, and Tick-Tock's rockers went 'Tick-Tock!' on the concrete which was, no doubt, his rocking-horse way of saying 'Thank you'.

The Adventures of Little Mouse

Once a mouse family lived under the floor of a play-room. There was a mother mouse and a father mouse. There was a big sister mouse called Mousikin and a baby brother mouse called Little Mouse.

They had a pleasant mouse-hole with two doors. One door opened into a toy cupboard in the play-room. The other opened into a long hall. Mother and father mouse ran down the long hall at night. They searched for crumbs or went into the kitchen to steal cheese. Mousikin and Little Mouse were not allowed to run in the hall. However, Mousikin was sometimes allowed to go into the toy cupboard. Little Mouse was too small to go anywhere. How he longed to see the world outside!

'What is the world like, Mousikin?' he would ask. 'Is it strange? Is it exciting? What smells are there in the world, Mousikin?'

'It is very strange out in the world, Little Mouse,' said Mousikin. 'The world is a lot of shelves one on top of the other. On the shelves are soft, staring creatures with round eyes. They do not blink or wink or even see anything. They don't smile or twitch their whiskers. They just sit there. They are called toys. There is a striped box, and if you open that box out leaps a little striped man – bang! And he grins at you. He is called Jack-in-the-box. There is a round red ball that would roll and bounce if there was room. There are blocks too. You can make mouse castles with them. The world smells of dust and rubber and books.'

'What are books, Mousikin?'

'Books are all sizes and colours, Little Mouse. You turn the pages. You look at the pictures. You grow wise and clever.'

'What does it mean to be wise, Mousikin?'

'It means to know all sorts of things, Little Mouse. It means to know why cheese smells so nice and how to tie a bell round the neck of a cat. It means to know how to bake bread or sing a song, or to know where sugar comes from.'

'Is it good to be wise, Mousikin?'

'It is the best thing in the world, Little Mouse. That is why I am teaching myself to read. I can read "A is for Apple, B is for Bear". I can read long words too.'

Little Mouse thought for a moment.

'Will you tell me the new words you learn, Mousikin? Then I will be wise too. I will be the wisest Little Mouse in the world.'

So Mousikin would come back from the toy cupboard and tell Little Mouse the new words she had learnt. Little Mouse learned 'A for Apple, B for Bear' too. He liked the long words best.

'What long words Little Mouse is saying now,' said Father Mouse proudly.

Then one day Mousikin came back from the toy cupboard, her black eyes round and shining.

'Oh, Little Mouse! Do you know what I saw today in the toy cupboard? I saw a picture in a book, Little Mouse. It was a picture of a huge monster, bigger than a cat, bigger than a dog . . . bigger even than a rocking-horse. Its name was the longest in the world. Its name – listen carefully, Little Mouse – its name was Brontosaurus.'

Little Mouse twitched his whiskers.

'Brontosaurus!' he said. 'That word is longer than I am.'

'It means Thunder Lizard, Little Mouse. This monster was so big it was called the Thunder Lizard. It had a long, long neck and a teeny-tiny

head. It had a great fat body and stumpy legs. Behind it was a tail as long as its neck.'

'Was its tail longer than my tail, Mousikin?' asked Little Mouse, who thought he had a very long tail indeed.

'Of course it was, you foolish Little Mouse. Its tail was longer than yours, longer than mine. It was longer than a piece of string. It was the tail of a monster.'

Little Mouse dreamed of the monster called Brontosaurus. He said its name over and over to himself. For two whole days he did not think of anything else but the Brontosaurus. He thought of its long neck and its teeny-tiny head. He thought of its tail.

'Brontosaurus means Thunder Lizard,' said Little Mouse to himself. He began to think of seeing the picture of the Brontosaurus for himself. 'I would like to see the picture of that Brontosaurus.'

Little Mouse asked to go to the toy cupboard with Mousikin.

'No, no, Little Mouse!' said his mother. 'You are too small.'

'If someone opened the cupboard door you would not know where to run to,' said Father Mouse. 'Children would catch you and put you in a cage. When you are older you can go with Mousikin.'

Little Mouse said nothing. He was making a special Little Mouse plan to go on his own, when no one was looking.

Next day when his parents were away and Mousikin was asleep Little Mouse stole out on his own. He wanted to get to the toy cupboard but he did not know the way. Down a dark passage he went, his whiskers prickling with excitement. He did not know where he was going. It was not the passage to the toy cupboard – it was the passage to the hall.

As he went Little Mouse heard a roar like thunder. Could it be a Brontosaurus roaring somewhere? He listened carefully. Then he went on very slowly. He came to the mouse-hole and peeped out. The mouse-hole was behind a big black chest in the hall. No one could see Little Mouse, but Little Mouse could see everything that was going on. The first thing he saw was a Brontosaurus.

Little Mouse knew it was a Brontosaurus because it had a long snaky neck and teeny-tiny head. It had a black tail too – a long, long tail. It was the longest tail Little Mouse had ever seen.

Someone was taking the Brontosaurus for a walk. Little Mouse could see a pair of feet walking beside it and a hand on its shiny neck. Its teeny-tiny head was flat on the ground. As it went by it roared like thunder and sucked up the dust. 'The Brontosaurus is a Thunder Lizard,' whispered Little Mouse softly. The whole world shook as the Brontosaurus went by.

Down at the end of the hall a door opened. Someone called out, 'Will you be much longer?'

'No,' said the owner of the feet that were taking the Brontosaurus for a walk. 'I will just put the vacuum cleaner away.' Someone picked the Brontosaurus up, and unplugged its tail from the wall. Someone carried the Brontosaurus away.

Little Mouse scurried back home down the mouse passage. How surprised his parents and Mousikin would be to hear how brave he had been.

'Mousikin, Mousikin! I have seen a real one. It is bigger than we ever thought and it really roars like thunder. Not only that, Mousikin, it eats dirt and dust for its tea. I saw it, Mousikin – and, Mousikin, it has another name. It is called Vacuum Cleaner.'

'Oh, Little Mouse!' said Mousikin. 'How wise you are now.'

'Yes,' said Father Mouse, 'but he should not have run away like that. Tomorrow you can go to the toy cupboard with Mousikin, but you must never go to the hall again. The Brontosaurus might get you next time.'

Little Mouse twitched his whiskers.

'Are you pleased, Little Mouse? Are you happy?' asked Mousikin.

Little Mouse smiled a mouse smile.

'I am so happy I feel as if all the world was cheese,' he said. And so he was.

The Boy Who Went Looking for a Friend

Once there was a little boy called Sam. He said to his mother, 'I am lonely. Where can I find a friend?'

His mother said, 'Behind our house is a field. It is filled with grass and red poppies and cornflowers. There are ears of wild wheat. There are big brown and yellow butterflies. Go into the field, Sam. Perhaps you will find a friend there.'

The little boy went into the field. Among the poppies and the grass he met a tiger. The tiger was

as yellow as sunshine. Over his coat were beautiful dark stripes. He had a very long twitching tail. 'Hallo, Tiger,' said Sam.

'Hallo, Sam,' said the tiger. He yawned a tiger yawn. His teeth looked very white. 'Are you the sort of tiger that eats boys?' asked Sam.

'No!' said the tiger. 'I only eat sandwiches. I have some sandwiches wrapped in lunch paper. Would you like some?' Sam and the tiger had a picnic on the grass. Then they played hide-and-seek all over the field. They hid up trees and behind trees, and made long secret tunnels through the grass. They had a lot of fun. But at sunset the tiger said, 'I must be going now.'

'Will you come back?' asked Sam.

'Perhaps I will,' said the tiger. 'Or perhaps I won't,' and off he went waving his tail.

Next day Sam said to his mother, 'I am lonely – where can I find a friend?'

His mother said, 'You know that tree down at the bottom of our garden. It is the tallest tree in the world. Its branches are so wide that sixteen wise monkeys could dance on them and there would still be room for you. You could put a table and chairs on its branches and eat your dinner there. Go to the tall tree, little Sam. You may find friends there.'

Off went Sam to the tall tree. There on its branches danced sixteen clever monkeys.

'Hallo, you monkeys!' called Sam. 'Can I climb up and dance with you?'

The monkeys made themselves into a long monkey-ladder and Sam climbed up it into the branches. On a big branch of the tree was a table and seventeen chairs. Sam and the monkeys sat down to eat. They ate pancakes and pineapple, sausages and strawberries. They drank raspberry juice out of long clear glasses. Then they all put on funny hats and laughed and sang. However, just as they were all having a lovely time the sun set. The monkeys started to climb the tree. They climbed much faster than Sam could.

'Where are you going to, monkeys?' he called.

'Higher up, higher up,' the monkeys squealed.

'Will you come back tomorrow?' asked Sam.

'Perhaps,' said the monkeys, 'or perhaps not.' Off they went, swinging by their tails.

Next day Sam said to his mother, 'I am lonely. Where can I find a friend?'

'Outside our gate,' said his mother, 'is a long road. It leads from a big town to a small town. It is dusty and grey. Along that road go all sorts of people. Some are in cars, some are on horses, some are on bicycles. Sometimes nobody goes by for a long time. But listen . . . I hear music on the road. Run and see, little Sam! It might be a friend.'

Sam heard the music and ran down to the gate.

'*Ta-ra-ra-ra!*' went the trumpet. '*Rat-a-plan-plan!*' went the drum. A circus was coming by. There were white horses and black horses. There were lions and elephants. There were packets of peanuts and pop-corn and a hundred hundred balloons. Best of all was Jimmy, the funny clown. The circus stopped.

'Here is Sam!' said Jimmy. 'Let's show him the circus.' The juggler juggled plates and cups and balls and balloons for Sam. He did not drop one. The elephants danced. A lovely fairy girl rode her white horse. She stood on its back, light as a feather, and did not fall off once. The men on the flying trapeze swung to and fro and tossed and turned in the air. Sam clapped and shouted. Most of all he laughed at Jimmy, the funny clown, riding his donkey backwards. Then it was sunset. The circus began to go on down the road.

'Where are you going?' called Sam.

'Farther on! Farther on!' called Jimmy the funny clown.

'Will you ever come back?' asked Sam.

'Perhaps we will, or perhaps we won't,' said Jimmy. Off they went round a bend in the road.

The next day Sam was too sad to ask his mother where he could find a friend.

'All my friends go away,' he thought. 'They all go to places where I can't go.' He went down to the river. He sat with his feet in the watercress. Then round a bend in the river came a little boat with a blue sail. It came past Sam. Then it stopped by the watercress and a boy got out. He was just Sam's size of boy, with an ordinary brown face and brown hair.

'Hallo!' he said. 'I didn't know you lived here. My name is Philip. What's your name?'

'Sam!' said Sam.

'Get in my boat and we will sail some more,' said Philip. They sailed all afternoon. Up and down the river bank they went, watching the fish in the clear green water. They saw wild ducks swimming and cows coming down to drink. They saw a wild, bright pheasant in the long grass. All the time they talked and made up stories. It was the best day of all. When it was sunset Philip said, 'We must go home now or our mothers will come calling us. May I come and play with you tomorrow, Sam? You are a good sort of friend to share my boat with me.'

'Of course,' said Sam, very pleased. 'We've had a good time, haven't we?'

'Tomorrow will be even better,' said Philip.

Sam went home and said to his mother, 'I've got a friend, Mother, and it isn't a tiger, and it isn't monkeys, and it isn't a circus. It's a boy called Philip.'

'That's good,' said his mother. 'Tigers are good friends for tigers. Monkeys are good friends for monkeys, and a circus is everybody's friend, but a boy is the best friend for a boy.'

'I didn't have to ask him to come and play tomorrow. He asked *me*,' said Sam.

'He sounds the best sort of friend then,' said Sam's mother.

'He wasn't in a field or up a tree or coming

down the road,' said Sam. 'I met him by the river.'

'Ah, now,' said Sam's mother, 'the river brings all things to those who wait.'

And this story is called, 'The Boy Who Went Looking for a Friend', and here is an end to it.

The Trees

Ever since Elizabeth could remember, pine trees had grown along the north fence like a line of giant green soldiers marching down the hill, but today, a bright shining blue and gold day, men were coming to cut them down.

Judith and Colin, who were both younger than Elizabeth, teased her at breakfast time. They were looking forward to the tree men coming with

their axes and saws and they could not understand why Elizabeth was not excited too. The
funny thing was Elizabeth could not explain it to
them.

'The trees will just *crash* down!' Colin cried.
'Like ninepins knocked over. Don't you even
want to hear them crash?'

'I'll hate it!' Elizabeth cried. She felt as if every
hair on her head was standing on end with anger.

'Why don't you want to hear it?' asked Judith,
looking at Elizabeth with a round solemn face
like a freckled owl.

'I just don't!' Elizabeth muttered. She wanted

to tell Judith that she loved the tall green pine trees. When she woke up in the morning and looked out of her window they were the first things she saw. Flying above them the magpies would toss and turn in the air making their strange silvery yodelling sound like a musical box gone wrong. When the moon crept over the sky at night Elizabeth saw it through the branches of the pines and that dark line of trees on the greeny brown hillside was her first sight of home when she came back from town. Because she had climbed them so often she felt she knew every branch and hollow of them by heart. They were all her friends, but the largest tree of all was her favourite because her swing hung from its lowest branch. Elizabeth was growing so tall that she had to tuck her feet under her when she was on the swing but she still loved swinging. Sometimes she felt the swing might come off and fly away with her to some magic land. It seemed terrible to think that after today she would never again swing high up and see blue sky through a criss-cross of branches and twigs and pine needles. Elizabeth wanted to explain this but somehow she didn't know the right words, and even if she did she felt Colin and Judith would not understand them.

'Anyhow,' Colin said, guessing her thoughts, 'Daddy says he'll make a new swing for us like one in the park.'

'That won't be the same,' Elizabeth said

scornfully. 'It will just be a dead *swing*. The one on the pine tree is alive.'

'You're as mad as mad!' Colin cried. 'Whoever heard of a live swing.'

Daddy looked at them crossly.

'Now you children!' he exclaimed. 'Stop that bickering and sniping. Elizabeth, *I'm* sorry the trees have to be cut down, too – they're seventy years old and were here when grandfather was born. But they've grown too tall – they're just not safe so close to the house any more. They've got to go. I'm not happy about it but there you are!'

'Yes, Daddy,' Elizabeth said, 'I know that,' and she tried to take no more notice of Colin and Judith, even when they whispered to each other watching her closely.

'Crash go the pine trees!'

Inside Elizabeth said to herself, 'It won't be like home ever again without the pine trees.'

After breakfast the tree fellers arrived in a truck. The back of the truck was loaded with axes and ropes and tins of lunch. And in the middle of all these things was a winch with wire rope wound round it. There were three tree fellers and they climbed out of the truck and shook hands with Elizabeth's father.

'Hallo!' said the tallest man of the three, looking at Judith and Colin. 'Have we got an audience?'

'They've been looking forward to it,' said Daddy. 'Whereas Elizabeth here wants us to keep the trees.' The tall man smiled at Elizabeth. He had white teeth and a brown crinkled face and he was wearing a blue shirt. Elizabeth liked him for a moment, then she thought to herself that he was a tree killer and she did not smile back.

'Will you chop the trees down with an axe?' asked Judith.

'No!' said the blue-shirt man. 'We'll use a chain saw.'

'Is that a saw to saw chains through?' Judith asked again, but of course she was only five and didn't know much.

'Don't be mad!' said Colin. 'It's a big saw with a motor on it, isn't it? You don't have to push and pull it – the motor drives it and makes it cut, doesn't it?'

'That's right,' said the blue-shirt man. 'I can see you know all about it. Now, let's have a look at these sticks!'

'Sticks!' Colin yelled. 'It's trees you've got to cut down – not sticks.'

'We call the trees sticks,' the blue-shirt man said. 'It stops us from being too frightened of them. It's dangerous cutting down trees, you know. They try to fall on us but we're too clever for them. We make them fall where we want them to.'

Elizabeth followed them as they all set off together to look at the trees.

'Sticks!' she thought. 'What a name for lovely green trees!' She watched with a mixed feeling of being interested and sad while the man fastened ropes to the first tree in the line. Then the blue-shirted man started up his chain saw. It roared like a lion until he cut into the tree with it. Then it screamed furiously and the sawdust flew out around the head and shoulders of the blue-shirt man. First he cut a piece out of one side of the tree and then he moved around to the other side where the chain saw screamed and the sawdust flew again. Then he stood back and shouted.

'All right – give her a go.'

The truck engine started up and moved forward by inches. The rope grew tight. Staring at the tree top Elizabeth saw it move as if there was a wind in it – a wind that the other pine trees could not feel. Then it started to fall. Elizabeth held her breath. It fell slowly at first, then fast and faster until it smashed on to the ground with a sound like crashing drums, thunder and tearing sheets. Branches broke. Pine cones flew into the air like startled birds. Judith and Colin screamed with delight.

'Didn't it crash! Gee! Didn't it crash!' yelled Colin.

'I thought it was scratching the sky down!' Judith cried. Elizabeth did not know what to say. It had been exciting to see the tree falling – to see all that great tower of needles, cones, and branches coming down at her (though of course it hadn't landed anywhere near her). Yet now there was a gap in the line of trees like a tooth missing in a smile. She felt sad again.

The chain saw screamed and the truck engine rumbled. Neighbours came to stare. Tree after tree came tumbling down. They lay in a great tangled mass of broken branches and oozing pine gum, smelling of the gum and bruised pine needles. They weren't part of a grand row of trees any more – they were just a mess.

Then it was lunch time. The men got their lunch tins and sat down to eat. Colin and Judith sat down beside them talking, while Elizabeth lurked a little way off, not wanting to join in, but not wanting to miss out on anything. Suddenly the blue-shirt man looked over Colin's head, straight at her.

'You're quiet today, lassie,' he said. 'So you're sorry to lose the trees!' Before Elizabeth could reply he went on: 'Think it's sad m'self to see those sticks come down, but some of them are old and tired, really dangerous. And don't you go thinking you're losing out altogether. You're losing the trees, sure, but look at the view. We're not just cutting down trees for your Dad – we're letting in the world.'

Elizabeth looked at the view. Up till now she had been just seeing it as a space where pine trees had been growing. Now she realized she could see right across the valley from her own hillside to the great greeny-brown hills opposite. In between lay farms and fields and the winding line of the creek with its fringe of poplars and willows. She could see the dark green shapes of the pine trees and firs, and the small white shapes of the sheep with their shadows beside them, short and stumpy because it was midday. Elizabeth had a feeling of space and sky she had never had before. Deep down inside her she knew that she would come to love this even more than she had loved her pine trees.

She looked at the blue-shirt man and smiled uncertainly.

During the afternoon when more of the trees came down Elizabeth looked at the widening space they left with a different feeling. She saw still more of the hills and the widening wandering creek come out from behind the pine trees. The new view was like a butterfly struggling out of its chrysalis – something gained not lost.

At last there was only the swing tree left. Elizabeth did not want to watch it fall. She went inside but all the time her ears were listening for the crash. It did not come. Instead she heard the truck starting up and going away again. When she looked out of the window she saw her new wide view and at the very end of it a single green soldier stood on guard – the swing tree.

Out ran Elizabeth into the kitchen where Colin and Judith were eating bread and jam. When Colin saw her he said:

'Anyhow, they didn't cut down your old swing tree, so there. It's still a strong tree and not anywhere near the house, so the blue-shirt man asked Daddy and Daddy said to leave it.'

'It was the biggest tree of all,' said Judith, but Elizabeth scarcely heard her. She ran out into the yard. It was not easy to get to the swing tree now, for the back of the yard was filled with the fallen pines, but Elizabeth wove her way over and under the grey trunks and branches. At last she stood under the old tree. She touched the swing dangling from it. She looked up at the sky through its branches and felt its rough bark under her hand.

'Hallo!' she said softly. 'Are you still here?' Then she got on the swing and worked her way up high sweeping backwards and forwards in a long swooping line. Above her the pine tree rustled and whispered as if it was talking to her. As she swung there she suddenly thought of the blue-shirt man and wished she had said thank you.

Patrick Comes to School

'Graham,' said the teacher, 'will you look after Patrick at play time? Remember he is new to the school and has no friends here yet.'

There were lots of things Graham would rather have done, but he had to smile and say, 'Yes, Mr Porter.'

Behind him Harry Biggs gave his funny, grunting laugh and whispered, 'Nursey-nursey Graham.' Mr Porter was watching so Graham could not say anything back.

Patrick was a little shrimp of a boy with red hair – not just carroty or ginger – a sort of fiery red. Freckles were all over his face, crowded like people on a five o'clock bus, all jostling and pushing to get the best places. In fact, Graham thought, Patrick probably had more freckle than face. As well as red hair and freckles, Patrick had a tilted nose and eyes so blue and bright that he looked all the time as if he'd just been given a specially good Christmas present. He seemed cheerful, which was something, but he was a skinny, short little fellow, not likely to be much good at sport, or at looking after himself in a fight.

'Just my luck to get stuck with a new boy!'
thought Graham.

At play time he took Patrick round and showed
him the football field and the shelter shed. Graham's friend Len came along too. Len and Graham were very polite to Patrick, and he was very
polite back, but it wasn't much fun really. Every
now and then Len and Graham would look at
each other over Patrick's head. It was easy to do,
because he was so small. 'Gosh, what a nuisance!'
the looks said, meaning Patrick.

Just before the bell went, Harry Biggs came up
with three other boys. Harry Biggs *was* big, and
the three other boys were even bigger, and came
from another class.

'Hallo, here's the new boy out with his nurse,'
said Harry. 'What's your name, new boy?'

Graham felt he ought to do something to protect little Patrick, but Patrick spoke out quite boldly and said, 'Patrick Fingall O'Donnell.' So that was all right.

Harry Biggs frowned at the name. 'Now don't be too smart!' he said. 'We tear cheeky little kids apart in this school, don't we?' He nudged the other boys, who grinned and shuffled. 'Where do you live, O'Donnell?'

Then Patrick said a funny thing. 'I live in a house among the trees, and we've got a golden bird sitting on our gate.'

He didn't sound as if he was joking. He spoke carefully as if he was asking Harry Biggs a difficult riddle. He sounded as if, in a minute, he might be laughing at Harry Biggs. Harry Biggs must have thought so too, because he frowned even harder and said, 'Remember what I told you, and don't be too clever. Now listen . . . what does your father do?'

'Cut it out, Harry,' said Graham quickly. 'Pick on someone your own size.'

'I'm not hurting him, Nursey!' exclaimed Harry. 'Go on, Ginger, what does he do for a crust?'

Patrick answered quickly, almost as if he was reciting a poem.

'My father wears clothes with gold all over them,' said Patrick. 'In the morning he says to the men, "I'll have a look at my elephants this morning," and he goes and looks at his elephants.

When he says the word, the elephants kneel down. He can ride the elephants all day if he wants to, but mostly he is too busy with the lions or his monkeys or his bears.'

Harry Biggs stared at Patrick with his eyes popping out of his head.

'Who do you think you're kidding?' he said at last. 'Are you making out your dad's a king or something? Nobody wears clothes with gold on them.'

'My father does!' said Patrick. 'Wears them every day!' He thought for a moment. 'All these lions and tigers lick his hands,' he added.

'Does he work in a circus?' asked one of the other boys.

'No!' said Patrick. 'We'd live in a caravan then, not a house with a golden bird at the gate.' Once again Graham felt that Patrick was turning his answers into riddles.

Before anyone could say any more the bell rang to go back into school.

'Gee, you'll hear all about that!' Len said to Patrick. 'Why did you tell him all that stuff?'

'It's true,' Patrick said. 'He asked me, and it's true.'

'He'll think you were taking the mickey,' Graham said. 'Anyway, it couldn't be true.'

'It *is* true,' said Patrick, 'and it isn't taking the mickey to say what's true, is it?'

'Well, I don't know,' Graham muttered to Len. 'It doesn't sound very true to me.'

Of course Harry Biggs and the other boys spread the story round the school.

Children came up to Patrick and said, 'Hey, does your father wear pure gold?'

'Not all gold,' said Patrick. 'Just quite a lot.'

Then the children would laugh and pretend to faint with laughing.

'Hey, Ginger!' called Harry Biggs. 'How's all the elephants?'

'All right, thank you,' Patrick would reply politely. Once he added, 'We've got a monkey too, at present, and he looks just like you.' But he only said it once, because Harry Biggs pulled his hair and twisted his ears. Patrick's ears were nearly as red as his hair.

'Serves you right for showing off,' said Graham.

'Well, I might have been showing off a bit,' Patrick admitted. 'It's hard not to sometimes.'

Yet, although they teased him, slowly children came to like Patrick. Graham liked him a lot. He was so good-tempered and full of jokes. Even when someone was laughing at him, he laughed too. The only thing that worried Graham was the feeling that Patrick was laughing at some secret joke, or at any rate at some quite different thing.

'Don't you get sick of being teased?' he asked.

'Well, I'm a bit sick of it now,' Patrick said, 'but mostly I don't mind. Anyhow, what I said was true, and that's all there is to say.'

'I'd hate to be teased so much,' Graham said. But he could see Patrick was like a rubber ball – the harder you knocked him down, the faster and higher he bounced back.

The wonderful day came when the class was taken to the Zoo. Even Harry Biggs, who usually made fun of school outings, looked forward to this one.

Off they went in the school bus, and Mr Porter took them round.

'. . . like the Pied Piper of Hamelin,' said Patrick, 'with all the rats following him.'

'Who are you calling a rat, Ginger?' said Harry Biggs sourly.

Everywhere at the Zoo was the smell of animals, birds and straw. They had a map which showed them the quickest way to go round the Zoo, and the first lot of cages they went past held birds. There were all sizes and colours of birds from vultures and canaries. One cage held several bright parrots. The parrots watched the children pass with round, wise eyes. Then suddenly the biggest and gayest of the lot flew from his perch and clung to the wire peering out at them.

'Patrick! Hallo, Patrick dear!' it said. 'Hallo! Hallo! Hallo, Patrick! Hallo, dear!'

Mr Porter looked at Patrick.

'Oh yes,' he said. 'I forgot about you, Patrick. It's a bit of a busman's holiday for you, isn't it?'

As they walked away the parrot went on screaming after them, 'Hallo, Patrick! Patrick! Hallo, dear!' in its funny, parrot voice.

On they went past the lions and tigers. Len and Graham stole sideways glances at Patrick, and so did Harry Biggs and several other children. Patrick looked as wide-eyed and interested as anyone else. He did not seem to see the glances at all.

They went past the bear pits, and then up a hill where there was nothing but trees. Among the trees, beside a stone fence, was a little house. On one of the gate posts was a brass peacock, polished until it shone, and below that was a little notice saying 'Head Keeper's Cottage'.

Now, for the first time, Patrick suddenly turned and grinned at Graham.

'*That*'s where I live,' he whispered.

They were all looking into the bear pits ten

minutes later when a man came hurrying to meet them. He was wearing a lot of gold braid all over his blue uniform. There was gold braid round his cap and his brass buttons shone like little suns. His eyes were blue and bright and his face was covered with freckles – more freckle than face you might have said. He stopped to speak to Mr Porter and took off his cap.

His hair was as red as fire.

'Is *that* your father?' Graham asked.

'Yes,' said Patrick. 'See, I told you he wore a lot of gold.'

'Huh!' said Harry Biggs. 'Well, why didn't you say when I asked you . . . why didn't you say he was a keeper at the Zoo?'

'Head Keeper!' said Graham, feeling suddenly very proud of Patrick.

'Ordinary keepers don't have gold,' Patrick pointed out.

'Why didn't you say?' Harry repeated. 'Trying to be clever, eh?'

'I don't like things to sound too ordinary,' said Patrick, sounding rather self-satisfied. 'I like them to be noble and sort of mysterious.'

'Well, you're mad,' said Harry, but no one was taking any notice of him. Mr Porter and Mr O'Donnell, Head Keeper, came back to them.

'This is Mr O'Donnell,' said Mr Porter. 'He has offered to let us have a look at the young lion cubs. They aren't on view to the public yet, so we are very lucky. And don't worry – the mother lion won't be there, so none of you will get eaten.'

As they went on their way a foolish little girl said to Patrick, 'Have you got any other relatives who do interesting things, Patrick?'

'Shut up!' said Graham, but it was too late.

'My uncle,' said Patrick without any hesitation. 'He's my great-uncle really, though. He eats razor blades for a living, razor blades and burning matches.'

'No one can eat razor blades!' shouted Harry Biggs.

'Well, my great-uncle does,' said Patrick, and this time everyone believed him.

PS. Patrick's great-uncle was a magician.

The Butterfly Garden

When Joan was on her own she had a secret game she liked to play. She had found a little place under the hedge where moss and leaves made a tiny green cave. It was too small for Joan to climb into, but it was just the right size for playing fairy gardens. Joan would go round and round the garden looking for something to make her green cave pretty. She would find thistledown, forget-me-nots and fallen petals from the flowers in Mother's garden. When she gathered enough Joan would go back to her tiny cave and decorate it with all the pretty things she had found.

'It's a fairy garden,' she told her mother. 'Come and see. It's a place for someone little to dance in. It looks really lovely now.'

The fairy gardens were always different, and for a while they did look pretty. In the spring Joan was allowed to pick a few violets. In the autumn there were crab apples and yellow poplar leaves. In the winter there were holly berries, although they were prickly to gather. However, the flowers faded and the berries withered and went wrinkly. Then Joan would have to make the garden all over again. It was part of the fun of it.

There was always one thing that worried Joan,

however. Did anyone use her pretty garden? Did fairy people truly come to dance there? Perhaps a family of frogs might come and sing or mice have a midnight picnic.

Joan did not really care who came into her garden as long as it was somebody small who would like to be there.

One morning Joan came running inside very excited.

'Mummy, Mummy!' she called. 'Someone has been in my garden. They've hung up a little lamp and then forgotten to take it down again.'

Mother and Joan went out to peer into the little

green cave. Hanging from the leafy roof was something that did look like a little green lantern with specks of gold in it.

'Dear me!' said Mother. 'It's a chrysalis.'

'Chrysalis' was a new word for Joan. She liked it because it was such a rich, unusual word. She said it twice, to enjoy the sound of it.

'Chrysalis . . . chrysalis . . . what's a chrysalis, Mummy?'

'Why,' said Mummy, 'it's a –' Then she stopped and laughed. 'You must wait and see. You may have to wait for a while but you will find out.'

For a few days Joan went to look at the chrysalis every morning, but it was not very interesting. It just hung there, always in the same place not changing at all. Sometimes Joan made a new little garden under it, being careful not to touch it. Sometimes she forgot it. Then, one day, at last she did find something different. The chrysalis was changing colour. It was getting darker.

'Mummy, it is getting ripe?' asked Joan, thinking of blackberries.

Mummy laughed. 'It's getting ready to change. You must watch it very carefully now.'

'Change what to?' asked Joan, but her mother just smiled.

The chrysalis turned black. Somewhere in it Joan could see a splash of red. She was really puzzled. What was the chrysalis up to?

She found out one warm, sunny day. Joan

looked into her garden and the chrysalis was gone, no, not quite gone, but quite changed. It had split open and was nothing but a little empty shape hanging from the leaves. Clinging to it with six long black legs was a new butterfly with red and black wings, looking as if he had just been painted. Slowly he opened and shut his wings, so Joan was able to see the wonderful bright pattern inside them. Mother came to look too.

'You see,' she said, 'it's a butterfly. The caterpillar must have crawled in from next door where Mrs Bates has the sort of plants caterpillars like to eat. This caterpillar must have thought your garden a nice safe place. He hung himself up here and changed into a chrysalis. All the time the chrysalis hung here he was inside, turning into a butterfly. Now he has broken out of the chrysalis and is ready to fly off and enjoy the summer. His wings will soon be strong enough.'

As Mother spoke the butterfly fluttered rather unsteadily out of the little green cave and on to

the hedge. He sat there for a moment, and then set off towards the flower beds.

'Well, I'm glad someone has used my garden,' Joan said. 'Every garden ought to have someone to live in it. Do you think that butterfly liked coming out and seeing my garden around him?'

'A special butterfly-sized garden!' said Mummy. 'I'm sure he did. Wouldn't you like it, if you were a butterfly?'

Billy Thring

One day Billy Thring decided to go adventuring, so he buttoned himself up and down in his new blue coat and set out with his lunch in his pocket. Now, on his way he met with a rat.

'Good morning, Rat! What are you at?' And the Rat answered . . .

'Trying to find a bacon rind.' So Billy Thring hastily said . . .

'If you come with me and be my travelling companion I will win you a bacon slice.'

Off they went together, wrapped up warm in the summer time.

The next person they met was a man playing the piano by the roadside, and all around him the meadows and fields laughed, their grassy hair full of flowers. Billy Thring said . . .

'It's a lovely day for a fellow to play.'

The Rat said . . .

'I like a song if it isn't too long.'

The Piano Player smiled like the sun and cried . . .

'I feel I'd be happy with folk such as you. So wherever you're going, I'll come along too.'

And he tucked his piano under his arm and

came with them. The next person they met was an old yellow toad.

Said Billy Thring . . .

'Good day to the Toad that sits in the road.'

Said the Rat . . .

'I like a fellow in old-cheese yellow.'

The Piano Player struck a fine note and sang . . .

'Doh, ray, mee, it's a prince I see.'

The Toad, much moved by their politeness, replied...

'Whatever you do, let me come too.'

Off they went, the four of them, talking about adventure. But this was not all, for soon they met a cock pheasant wearing a crown.

Billy Thring said...

'This bird has the dress of a king, no less.'

The Rat squeaked...

'His eyes have the spark of a fire in the dark.'

The Piano Player sang...

'His tail is as long as a verse of my song.'

The Toad croaked...

'For beauty and grace he must take first place.' Utterly delighted with these elevated sentiments the Pheasant cried...

'Friendly words are be-
loved by birds. You are
but four and you need one
more.'

And so they went on
their way all five of them
. . . Billy Thring, the Rat,
the Piano Player, the
Toad and the Pheasant in
its golden crown.

Then in a secret woodland place they came
upon a Green Man dancing on goat feet with a
Green Girl. They danced and danced, but they
looked so sad that Billy Thring paused and asked
them what was wrong.

'Our castle has been stolen,' they said. 'For
years we have lived in a castle over the hill. Now
robbers have taken it from us, stealing it when we
were at our moonlight dancing.'

'Ah, we will fix that!' Billy Thring told them.
Off the companions went over the hill, and there
they saw a castle of bright stone. Robbers of all
sizes looked out of every window.

'Now I shall begin,' the Pheasant said. The
Piano Player played and the Pheasant danced
gracefully. The robbers saw its golden crown.
'We must have that,' they said to each other and
came out from the castle. Unseen by them the
Toad hopped in and went to the big, black cannon over the gateway. The Piano Player played a
sleepy tune. The robbers stopped, and each stood

on one leg and tucked his head under his arm like a sleepy bird as they listened to the lullaby. Only the robber chief stayed awake.

'Seize that Piano Player!' he roared, but nobody did.

The Rat and Billy Thring attacked the robbers. The Rat nipped them – they tasted like bacon. Billy Thring struck them with his fists.

But . . . there were too many robbers. Too many, too many! They were beating Billy Thring and the Rat. Then the Piano Player hit the robber chief with his piano, and the Toad fired the cannon. BOOM! When the smoke cleared away all the robbers were dead.

'Good,' said Billy Thring. 'Get the Green Dancers.'

The Green Dancers came back, and with them came the Horned Men, the Bird Women, lizards with eyes like tiny jewels, butterflies and beetles. Flowers twined, grapes ripened on the vine, the sun and moon danced hand in hand across the sky, and the stars sang with voices of honey. Furry people blew trumpets, the walls of the castle fell out, and the forest came gladly in.

'Our true castle has no walls but the trees, no ceiling but the sky!' the Green Dancers cried.

'I shall take rooms for my friends and myself,' said Billy Thring promptly. 'The Piano Player will give you our rent in songs. We've had the glory. Now we will have the gladness.'

They lived for ever in the forest, ate and drank, danced and sang, told stories, slept and woke up each day with new delight. The Rat, the Piano Player, the Toad and the Pheasant were very happy, but the happiest of all was Billy Thring.

Tom Tib Goes Shopping

Little Tom Tib could stand on his head and walk on his hands. He could whistle like a blackbird and swim like a fish. In fact there were lots of things he could do, but there was one thing he could not do, try as he might. He could not remember what mother told him to buy at the shops.

She told him to get bread, and he came back with a green umbrella. She told him to get butter, and he came back with a sugar sack full of Easter eggs. She told him to get a bottle of vinegar, and he came home with a baby elephant.

'Where on earth did you get *that*?' his mother asked him, but Tom Tib could not remember.

That was the way with Tom Tib. He could remember his nine-times table, he could remember to wash his knees – a thing a lot of boys forget to do – but he could not remember what he was supposed to buy at the shops.

'Tom Tib, Tom Tib,' said his mother. 'What can I do with a baby elephant? I won't send you to the shop ever again.'

'Let me try once more,' Tom Tib begged, and he begged and pleaded and wheedled so hard that his mother finally said,

'Very well, you can try once more, but this is your last chance. I would like you to get me a pot of honey. Now, so that you will remember, I will tell you this little rhyme:

> Isn't it sticky, isn't it sweet?
> Just what a big bear loves to eat.'

Tom Tib said the rhyme over and over to himself until he knew it by heart. Then he went off to the shop singing it as he went.

Now, as it happened, on his way to the shop he met with a really, truly, big bear. This big bear was in sad trouble. He had stolen a tin from somebody's shed thinking it might have honey in it. He had opened the tin and pushed his nose into it. Alas, the tin was full of paint. The bear got paint in his eyes and mouth, and the tin stuck on his nose and wouldn't come off.

As the bear was struggling with the tin Tom Tib went by singing his rhyme:

> 'Isn't it sticky, isn't it sweet?
> Just what a big bear loves to eat.'

This made the bear so cross that he jerked with his paws, and the tin flew off:

'Foolish boy!' snarled the bear. 'You should say:

> When in doubt
> Keep your nose OUT.'

Now, the next person he met was a rose-grower, a man who loved growing roses. He had just grown the loveliest red rose you ever saw. He was so excited that when he saw Tom Tib coming down the road he called, 'Look at my rose. I say, look at my rose! Come here and I'll let you smell it, little lad.'

But Tom Tib was busy trying to remember what it was he had to get at the shop, and he pranced along singing:

> 'When in doubt
> Keep your nose OUT.'

The rose-grower was dreadfully annoyed. 'Rude boy!' he screamed. 'Listen! If somebody asks you to admire their beautiful red rose you should say:

> What a truly wonderful smell, and
> What a lovely red, as well.'

Immediately Tom Tib forgot the bear's rhyme. He went on dancing along the road singing the words that the rose-grower had told him to say.

Round the corner he came on a very strange sight indeed. Old Mr Finn had thrown his rubbish out over the hedge. He did not look to see if anyone was passing by, and the rubbish had gone all over Mrs Fat in her new silk dress and her tall straw hat.

Poor Mrs Fat, all dirty and grey with dust. She

had eggshells and fishbones in her hair, and she smelled of fish too. Just then Tom Tib danced by singing:

> 'What a truly wonderful smell, and
> What a lovely red as well.'

Mrs Fat hit Tom Tib with her umbrella.

'Are you making fun of me, Tom Tib?' she cried. 'I'll skin you, I'll boil you, I'll bake you in butter! What you ought to say is:

> I'm terribly sorry to see such a mess,
> Over your shoulders, over your dress!'

Straight away Tom Tib changed his song, without really knowing that he had changed it. Off he went and at last he came to the shop. There, on a stool by the shop door sat Daffodil, the shopkeeper's daughter, combing her golden hair, and beside her was Nobby the carpenter nailing up a new step for the shop.

Up came Tom Tib, cheerful as a cricket, and, taking one look at Daffodil's long and tumbling golden hair, he sang:

> 'I'm terribly sorry to see such a mess,
> Over your shoulders, over your dress.'

Nobby the carpenter looked up from his work.

'Tom Tib,' he said, 'you'll never get far if you

say things like that to a pretty girl combing her hair. What you should say is:

> Sweetest gold from here to home
> Keep it nice and use a comb.'

That was enough for Tom Tib. He forgot Mrs Fat's words and could remember only Nobby's.

'Now, Tom Tib,' said the shopkeeper, 'what is it you want today? We're out of elephants, you know.'

'Oh, it's not an elephant,' Tom Tib said. 'At least I don't *think* so. I can't quite remember. But my mother told me a rhyme to help me remember it. Listen!

> Sweetest gold from here to home
> Keep it nice and use a comb.'

'Why,' said the shopkeeper, '*that*'s easy, your mother wants a pot of honey.'

'So she does!' said Tom Tib. 'I remembered the rhyme, didn't I?'

Tom Tib's mother was delighted when he turned up with the honey.

'Well, you must be improving,' she said. 'How clever of you to remember my rhyme all the way to the shop!'

'Perhaps I *was* a bit clever,' said Tom Tib, looking pleased.

But which do *you* think was the clever one?

The Little Boy Who Wanted a Flat World

There was once this little boy sitting in the back of a class at school, listening to a teacher. The teacher had a globe of the world on her desk and was talking to the children about it.

'Once upon a time,' she said, 'men thought the world was flat, but now we know it is round, just like the globe here.'

The little boy looked at the globe, but he wasn't at all pleased with it. In his mind he imagined the world as quite flat, with all the seas pouring over the edge of it, down and down, smooth as glass, down through space, rustling between the stars. He liked the idea of a flat world so much better than a round one, just as he liked glass castles and unicorns and mermaids singing.

'All nice things are pretendings,' he thought. 'None of them are real.' And he went on feeling sorry that the world was round all day.

He was a very little boy you see.

That very night the little boy woke up, feeling the dark grow suddenly warm around him. He found he was lying in long grass in the sunshine.

He was not as surprised as you might think, though he was rather dismayed to find himself in such gaily coloured clothes . . . and not ordinary clothes at that. He seemed to be wearing a short skirt and long stockings, and his hair was long too. Then, along came a group of other children and he saw that the boys were dressed just as he was, and the little girls wore dresses down to their ankles.

'Well,' he thought, 'I have got myself into a long-ago time when people dressed differently.' He didn't bother about his clothes any more, but felt happy again. He joined in with them, and off they went down a stony, bumpy street chasing pigeons and talking away to each other.

As they went on their noisy, chattering way they came upon a tall, lean man by the roadside, sitting with his chin on his knees.

'Look, it's Wilkin,' the children cried, crowding around him. 'Tell us a story, Wilkin! Sing us a song!'

Wilkin had a torn blue cloak and a blue tunic. His solemn dark face suddenly broke into smiles. He put his arm around the youngest child and he sang.

'I woke in the morning and looked at the day.
I saw it was asking that I should be gay
So dancing I went with a leap and a bound,
And a song as glad as the world is round.'

'But the world isn't really round, silly Wilkin!' said a little child. 'It's as flat as a penny, and the sea falls over the edge.'

So then the little boy knew that somehow he had woken up in that long time ago when the world was flat.

'But last night,' Wilkin told the children, 'I had a dream. I dreamed I was out in the sky – far, far, far out, where the stars hold their small bright lamps. And so you know what – I could see our world, and it was quite round. Round like a little shining jewel, a spark of glowing fire. When I flew closer I could see the blue sea on it, and the lands like green and brown patches. I saw these things through the streaks of drifting cloud. Yes, and I could see day and night chasing each other round the world, and ships sailing and sailing and coming back to where they started, and I thought what a beautiful world it was, and how wonderful it would be if it were really round. Why, just think – I could start off from here and run like lightning, leap from wave to wave, step over forests and lakes and mountains, and be back here again before you could wink. But with a flat world I'd just fall over the edge.'

Then all the children laughed.

'No one can run from land to land,' said one, 'and anyway the world is flat.'

'There is no other country over the sea,' said one, 'but only strange monsters that will eat you, Wilkin.'

'The world is flat, Wilkin,' cried a third.

'The world is flat,' Wilkin repeated sadly. 'And all poetry is dust.' The little boy saw that Wilkin was disappointed at seeing his bright dreams burst like bubbles on the children's pinprick words, so he moved closer to Wilkin and pulled his sleeve.

'Really, the world is round,' he whispered, and he and Wilkin smiled a secret smile at each other.

At that moment far away the little boy heard someone call his name. He turned to look over his

shoulder, and saw the wallpaper of his own room. He had been in bed dreaming.

Later, as the little boy ate his breakfast, he asked his mother, 'Which is it most beautiful for worlds to be . . . flat or round?'

'It depends,' his mother answered, 'on what you think yourself.'

'I think round worlds are quite nice after all,' the little boy said thoughtfully. He smiled to himself and went on eating his breakfast.

The Strange Egg

Once Molly found a strange leathery egg in the swamp. She put it under Mrs Warm the broody hen to hatch it out. It hatched out into a sort of dragon.

Her father said, 'This is no ordinary dragon. This is a dinosaur.'

'What is a dinosaur?' asked Molly.

'Well,' said her father, 'a long time ago there were a lot of dinosaurs. They were all big lizards. Some of them were bigger than houses. They all died long ago . . . All except this one,' he added gloomily. 'I hope it is not one of the larger meat-eating lizards as then it might grow up to worry the sheep.'

The dinosaur followed Mrs Warm about. She scratched worms for it, but the dinosaur liked plants better.

'Ah,' said Molly's father. 'It is a plant-eating dinosaur – one of the milder kind. They are stupid but good-natured,' he added.

Professors of all ages came from near and far to see Molly's dinosaur. She led it around on a string. Every day she needed a longer piece of string. The dinosaur grew as big as ten elephants. It ate all the flowers in the garden and Molly's mother got cross.

'I am tired of having no garden and I am tired of

making tea for all the professors,' she said. 'Let's send the dinosaur to the zoo.'

'No,' said Father. 'The place wouldn't be the same without it.'

So the dinosaur stayed. Mrs Warm used to perch on it every night. She had never before hatched such a grand successful egg.

One day it began to rain . . . It rained and rained and rained and rained so heavily that the water in the river got deep and overflowed.

'A flood, a flood – we will drown,' screamed Molly's mother.

'Hush, dear,' said Molly's father. 'We will ride to a safe place on Molly's dinosaur. Whistle to him, Molly.'

Molly whistled and the dinosaur came towards her with Mrs Warm the hen, wet and miserable, on his back. Molly and her father and mother climbed on to the dinosaur's back with her. They held an umbrella over themselves and had warm drinks out of a thermos flask. Just as they left, the house was swept away by the flood.

'Well, dear, there you are,' said Molly's father. 'You see it was useful to have a dinosaur, after all. And I am now able to tell you that this is the biggest kind of dinosaur and its name is Brontosaurus.'

Molly was pleased to think her pet had such a long, dignified-sounding name. It matched him well. As they went along they rescued a lot of other people climbing trees and house tops, and floating on chicken crates and fruit boxes. They rescued cats and dogs, two horses and an elephant which was floating away from a circus. The dinosaur paddled on cheerfully. By the time they came in sight of dry land, his back was quite crowded. On the land policemen were getting boats ready to go looking for people, but all the people were safe on the dinosaur's back.

After the flood went down and everything was as it should be, a fine medal was given to Molly's dinosaur as most heroic animal of the year and many presents were given to him.

The biggest present of all was a great big swimming-pool made of rubber so you could blow it up. It was so big it took one man nearly a year to blow it up. It was a good size for dinosaurs of the Brontosaurus type. He lived in the swimming-pool after that (and Molly's mother was able to grow her flowers again). It is well known that Brontosauruses like to swim and paddle. It took the weight off his feet. Mrs Warm the hen used to swim with him a bit, and it is not very often you find a swimming hen.

So you see this story has a happy ending after all, which is not easy with a pet as big as ten elephants. And just to end the story I must tell you that though Molly's dinosaur had the long name of Brontosaurus, Molly always called it 'Rosie'.

A Tall Story

Susan was the family story-teller, and Richard was the family listener. She told the stories and he always listened.

But when Uncle Ted came to call, it turned out he was a story-teller too, and Richard stopped listening to Susan. He listened to Uncle Ted all the time, one story after another.

'Tell a story, Uncle Ted!' demanded Richard.

'Don't start him off again,' begged Susan. 'I think it's bad to encourage him.'

'Just one little story,' Richard begged.

Uncle Ted leaned back, looked up at the ceiling, as story-tellers do.

'I think I've told most of my stories,' he said. 'Let me see! I've told you about the mystery treasure of Bones Island, haven't I?'

'That was a good one,' Richard answered, smiling and remembering.

'Oh yes . . . and I've told you about the time I was nearly married to the Queen of the Bird People?'

'She lived in a big royal nest, didn't she?' Richard nodded. 'And laid eggs.'

'What about the catching of the Great Christmas Tree Thieves – a smart bit of detective work on my part?' Uncle Ted asked, thinking hard. 'All the thieves were dressed as Santa Claus.'

'Hasn't anything happened to you since then?' Richard asked.

'Nothing, nothing,' said Uncle Ted sadly. 'Except, of course, for the hunting of the giant land-dwelling oyster. You'll remember the headlines in the paper, no doubt. You may even have seen it on TV.'

'You don't hunt oysters,' Susan said snappily. 'You fish for them. You know you fish for them, Uncle Ted.'

'Those are the small ones,' Uncle Ted replied carelessly. 'This was a large one . . . enormous! . . . a horrible amorphous creature as big as a town hall . . . a land-dwelling oyster.'

'It couldn't be,' Susan said sternly. 'No oyster could be as big as a town hall.'

'Tell me!' begged Richard. 'Tell a story.'

So Uncle Ted began: 'This dreadful monster had taken to coming out at night, and snatching up all kinds of midnight travellers. Five vans of buns and assorted sweets on their way to a southern carnival had vanished off the face of the earth. Two brass bands, a travelling circus, a mobile library and an army lorry filled with angry sergeant-majors had entirely disappeared . . . We couldn't let it continue. A creature with a digestion like that had to be got rid of. No one was safe – not even town councillors. Of course, they sent for me, offering to pay richly if I disposed of the monster.'

Uncle Ted paused.

'You always make adventures pay,' said Richard. 'Go on.'

'None of it is true,' Susan muttered.

'I chose three guns . . . my trusty revolver, my trusty 303 rifle, and my trusty 1812 cannon. I drove towards the giant oyster's lair in my little truck with the hotted-up engine. Many oyster soup officials were standing by, with a Pre-Fabricated Re-Locatable Oyster-Soup factory. As soon as I had shot the giant oyster they would move in with a hundred oyster-soup cooks, great vats of salt and pepper, and bags of lemons. They hoped to make a year's supply of oyster soup from this dreadful monster.'

'I'll bet you planned all that,' said Richard. 'Were you getting money for it?'

'I was to get ten cents for every tin of oyster

soup. They expected to sell at least twenty tins of soup a day over a year. It was a small fortune,' said Uncle Ted.

'Uncle Ted, nobody believes you,' said Susan, shaking her head.

Uncle Ted went on: 'I moved in first with a loudspeaker. From a distance of a mere two hundred yards I began making sarcastic remarks about oysters. This was to infuriate the oyster and bring it out into the daylight. Out it came . . . a great amorphous mass as big as a town hall.'

'You've already said that,' objected Susan.

'Was it horrible?' asked Richard.

'Unspeakably horrible!' Uncle Ted cried, shuddering. 'It reared up menacingly over the trees, all slimy and jelly-like with great teeth gnashing in a wide slit of a mouth.'

'Oysters don't have teeth,' Susan stated.

'They don't usually,' agreed Uncle Ted. 'I can't explain it. I'm not an oyster expert. All I know is, this oyster came undulating towards me at surprising speed, gnashing a mouthful of very sharp-looking teeth. Perhaps it had made itself some false teeth out of oyster shell.'

'I don't know how you can bear to listen to such things,' Susan muttered to Richard, shaking her head again.

'I fired first with my trusty 303 rifle, and then with my trusty revolver. I could not miss such a huge target, but mere bullets made no difference. Even when I fired the cannon ball right through it,

it did not hesitate. I had to climb into my truck and drive off as quickly as I could.'

'But the oyster could catch trucks!' cried Susan triumphantly. 'You said it had caught an army lorry.'

'Too true!' agreed Uncle Ted. 'It nearly caught up with me, but my truck, though small, was fitted with an experimental jet engine of a revolutionary kind. Just as the oyster (a vast amorphous mass, did I mention?) was about to swoop on me, I pressed button A and rotating helicopter blades unfolded out of the roof of my truck, whisking me out of danger. Furious at losing its prey, the terrible mollusc set up a wailing so horrible that –

I give you my word – the helicopter blades nearly stopped, and I hung quivering in the air. There were a few tense moments, believe me, before I got back out of reach and the oyster gave up and slunk back to its cave.

'There was great despondency when I returned at last.

'"We'll have to declare a national emergency and call out the army," declared the town councillors. The oyster soup officials weren't too happy about this. The army could deal with it, of course, but this meant blowing the monster to bits – thus spoiling it for soup purposes. The oyster soup officials didn't fancy picking bits of oyster out of the trees for miles around.

'We all thought hard. A quick, cool brain is worth a million in an emergency.

' "I've got a plan," I said. "It'll cost a bit to get it under way, and if it works I'll want fifteen cents on every can of oyster soup."

' "You drive a hard bargain," said the leading oyster soup official. "But we have no choice. If we get this great oyster, I think we'll manage to get command of the entire oyster-soup market."

'Now,' cried Uncle Ted, 'what do you think my plan was?'

'I couldn't ever guess,' said Susan sourly. 'It could be anything.'

'Go on, Uncle Ted,' whispered Richard, staring at Uncle Ted anxiously.

'All afternoon we spent loading a council dust and refuse truck. The hotel gave us five kegs of beer – rather a poor brew, I'm afraid. Miss Dobbs, the vicar's sister, hearing the announcement of our plan over the radio, contributed a whole dozen bottles of her famous parsnip-and-elderberry wine. Several farmers gave large quantities of apple cider. Colonel Scobie donated several flagons of a drink of his own invention – carrot whisky, he called it. He said it helped him see in the dark, being extra rich in Vitamin A . . .

A Japanese family gave us a cask of saki – I think that's made from rice. My gift was simple, but incredibly rich – simply five cases of simple French champagne that I happened to have with me.'

'Uncle Ted, your stories are all lies and boasting,' cried Susan. 'Lies! Lies!'

'Susan,' said her mother, 'you are not to call your uncle a liar. Go outside if you can't behave better.'

Susan went outside. 'Uncle or not, it's still all lies,' she told the cat. Then she hid in the garden under the open window to listen to the rest of the story.

Inside the house Uncle Ted was going on: 'Who was to drive this truck? Every eye looked hopefully at me. It was putting my head into the jaws of death yet again, but I agreed with a tired smile. We travelling adventurers are prepared for anything. Besides, I had a small fortune at stake.

'Late that night I drove the truck down the road that passed by the oyster's lair. As we had expected the oyster charged out at the lorry. I saw its dark shape against the stars – a vast amorphous mass (as I just may have mentioned before) and I had time to slide out and hide in a ditch while the oyster, not realizing I had gone, swept by me and devoured the truck . . . beer, carrot whisky, cider, parsnip wine, saki, champagne and all.

'We waited anxiously. After about a quarter of an hour the oyster began to behave in a very strange fashion. It began to sway to and fro and actually tried to sing. I can tell you, it was one of the worst half-hours of my career. I've sat through operas and many folksong recitals, but nothing, nothing to compare with the giant oyster, full of champagne and carrot whisky, trying to sing. It was drunk, of course.'

'An oyster drunk!' cried Richard, almost not believing.

'Hopelessly inebriated!' Uncle Ted said solemnly. 'At the end of half an hour it collapsed in a quivering heap. The Pre-Fabricated Re-Locatable Oyster-Soup factory came in, the cooks got to work and – well – you're having some of it for dinner tonight, so your mother tells me.'

'Was it fair to cut it up while it was helpless?' asked Richard doubtfully.

'Not quite fair – but you can't consider fair play too strongly when you're dealing with a creature that will tackle a lorry full of sergeant-majors, you know. Besides, it must have died happy – don't forget it had just consumed a year's supply of French champagne. People tasting the soup, incidentally, comment on the delicate champagne flavour that complements the oyster so beautifully. Go out into the kitchen, and get your mother to show you the genuine tin.'

Richard ran off, and Uncle Ted could hear him shouting excitedly in the kitchen.

'Uncle Ted,' said a voice, and there was Susan. 'Uncle Ted, shall I tell you how the story really ended?'

Uncle Ted looked at her cautiously. 'I'd like to hear,' he said.

Susan began: 'There you were, driving down the road at midnight. You saw the oyster descending on the truck . . . a vast amorphous mass –'

'I like the words you choose,' interrupted Uncle Ted.

'Now, *now* was the time for you to leap out of the truck. You went to open the door. Horrors! it was locked. It was a special automatically locking door, easy to open if you knew the way, but you had forgotten to check up. The giant oyster was coming nearer and nearer and then – and then . . .'

'Yes! Yes!' whispered Uncle Ted.

'Alas, the monster leaped on to the truck and ate you all up. You struggled wildly but it was no use. Later you were turned into soup and Mother is cooking you in the kitchen right now.'

'But I seem to be still here,' objected Uncle Ted. 'I'm sure I'm here . . .'

'All ghosts feel that,' Susan said firmly. 'I'm afraid, Uncle Ted, you are a mere ghostly apparition.'

Uncle Ted and Susan looked at each other . . . They began to smile. They began to laugh.

'A much better end,' said Uncle Ted. 'I didn't

realize there was another tall-story-teller in the family.'

'It's not really a better end, just a bit taller,' said Susan. 'Yours can be the right one. You laugh too hard for a ghost! Now you tell your end to the story specially for me.'

'I think it's time you told me a story,' said Uncle Ted. 'For instance, I've heard all sort of rumours about the time you were carried off by the rare Subterranean Gorilla, who had seen you swimming at the beach and had been much struck by your remarkable beauty. Wouldn't you like to tell me the facts of the case? You might have time before the soup is served?'

So Susan told him that story and, as it turned out, Uncle Ted was a wonderful listener – all good story-tellers have to be – even better than Richard.

C.E. MURPHY

HOUSE·OF CARDS

LUNA™

www.LUNA-Books.com

LUNA™

Recycling programs
for this product may
not exist in your area.

HOUSE OF CARDS

ISBN-13: 978-0-373-80311-8

www.LUNA-Books.com

Printed in U.S.A.

Author's Note

"Where," comes the dreaded question, "do you get your ideas?"

The Negotiator trilogy originally sprang from a *Beauty and the Beast*-with-gargoyles idea a friend and I discussed. The resemblance between that initial discussion and the story you're now reading is pretty much imperceptible. Well, there were gargoyles in the original idea, so I suppose it's perceptible, but only just.

I came back to the idea a couple of years later, having realized that if there were gargoyles, there were probably other nonhuman races littering the planet, as well, and that an interesting way to learn about them would be to put an ordinary human woman in their midst. Margrit Knight arrived fully formed in my head one morning, and from there I essentially never looked back. (I rewrote a lot, but I never looked back!) Discovering her world and embroiling her in the Old Races' politics has been a fantastic journey for me. I hope you enjoy it as much as I have!

Catie